D1375900

ARE YOU BRAVE ENOUGH

TO START THE

CREEPER FILES?

THEY'RE PRETTY SCARY . . .

NOW WHERE DID I PUT MY

BUG SPRAY . . .

YOU HAVE BEEN

WARNED . . .

The ground heaved with thousands of spiders. They scrambled and scampered over each other, writhing and scurrying across the path in all directions.

The street lights returned, flooding the garden with light. Sarah couldn't tear her eyes from the mass of arachnids all around her, but Jake and Liam both looked up at the lamps. The darkness that had been covering them wasn't paint. It was spiders! Thousands of spiders had been blocking out the lights!

All along the street, the army of creepy-crawlies released their grips and dropped away from the glass. They fell lightly to the ground, and Jake imagined them closing in from all directions, racing towards the garden.

'Move!' he yelped, turning and racing towards the door. He was fumbling with the keys when disaster struck! He tripped, stumbled, and the keys slipped from his fingers. They landed right in the middle of the path, and were immediately buried by the heaving carpet of arachnids.

'No!' Sarah cried.

'I'll get them!' said Liam. He thrust his hand into the squirming mass and eight or more of the arachnids immediately began clambering up his arm.

Sarah and Jake hopped up onto the front step. There were fewer of the bugs here, and they frantically slapped at their legs, trying to knock away the dozens of spiders climbing up them.

'Get them off! Get them off!' Sarah squealed, thrashing and kicking. Jake cleared the spiders off his own legs, then turned his attention to helping Sarah.

Liam charged at them, thrusting the keys at Jake. His arms and neck were covered in creepy-crawlies. As soon as Jake grabbed the keys, Liam spun on the spot, scratching and clawing at himself to get the bugs off.

'Not so fast, you eight-legged freaks!' Liam yelped, flicking four or five particularly large specimens off the front of his T-shirt. He caught another one before it could climb into his ear, although what it was planning to get up to in there, he had no idea. Nothing good, probably.

Jake got the door open and the three friends tumbled inside. As soon as Sarah and Liam were safely in, Jake slammed the door behind them, and locked it, for good measure. He was pretty sure spiders couldn't operate door handles, but it wasn't a chance he was willing to take.

OXFORD
UNIVERSITY PRESS

Great Clarendon Street, Oxford OX2 6DP

Oxford University Press is a department of the University of Oxford.
It furthers the University's objective of excellence in research, scholarship,
and education by publishing worldwide. Oxford is a registered trade mark
of Oxford University Press in the UK and in certain other countries

British Library Cataloguing in Publication Data

Data available

ISBN: 978-0-19-274734-1

1 3 5 7 9 10 8 6 4 2

Printed in Great Britain

Paper used in the production of this book is a natural,
recyclable product made from wood grown in sustainable forests.
The manufacturing process conforms to the environmental
regulations of the country of origin.

HACKER MURPHY'S

CREEPER FILES

INCY WINCY... EEK!

OXFORD
UNIVERSITY PRESS

the Larkspur

EIGHT-LEGGED FREAK!

Large spider stows away in supermarket bananas

By our man in town,
HACKER MURPHY

Local woman, Angie Paul, received a nasty shock this week, when she unpacked her supermarket shopping to find a spider nestled in a bunch of bananas. But this was no ordinary spider. Instead, it was a spider that was slightly larger than normal size!

Angie, 42, had just tipped all the old, black, uneaten bananas from her fruit bowl in her bin, and was about to replace them with the fresh bunch when she made the horrifying discovery.

'Horrible, it was,' said Angie, visibly shaken by the encounter. 'It had, like, eight legs, a big fat body, and I swear,

Chronicle

you could see all its hairs and its eyes,' before adding, 'You know, if you'd had a microscope or whatever.'

The spider, which was believed to have been anything up to four centimetres long before Angie's husband, Malcolm, hit it with a shoe, is just one of a number of recent arachnid-related incidents to happen in the Larkspur area.

Experts believe that the wet but mild September has led to an increase in the local spider population, with some claiming the Larkspur area may be about to witness 'a spider epidemic' the like of which hasn't been seen in

CHAPTER ONE

HACKER'S WELCOME

Hey there. Hacker Murphy here, bringing you the story behind the story.

If you've read some of my other Creeper Files, you know the drill by now. If not, allow me to introduce myself. I'm a reporter for The Larkspur Chronicle, one of those local newspapers that cover all the BIG stories. Whether it's a detailed recounting of a ten-hour council meeting, a thrilling exposé of the laundrette's new opening hours, or an explosive opinion piece on local car parking facilities, you'll find it all in the Chronicle.

You'll wish you hadn't, obviously, but you'll find it.

But there's more to Larkspur than the Chronicle

would have you believe. Much as I'd love to reveal the truth in my articles, my editor refuses to let me. He thinks either I'm making it all up, or am completely delusional.

He is wrong.

You see, a monster lurks in Larkspur. He takes on many guises, and wears many faces, but the few people who know about him refer to him by just one name: The Creeper!

And sometimes by his real name, Woody Hemlock, but the 'just one name' bit sounded more dramatic.

Not that drama's ever in short supply when the Creeper is around. He's a plant-controlling, nature-manipulating, full-scale-crazy monster who alternates between trying to rule the world and trying to destroy it.

Fortunately for the rest of us, three local children have so far been able to stop him. After their last encounter, they'd hoped to have seen the last of the Creeper, but the Creeper, as usual, had other ideas.

But back to 'the story behind the story'. That article I've included in this file about the large (well, large-ish) spider sighting is 100% true. Angie Paul did, in fact, find an above-average-sized spider in her bananas.

What I didn't mention, though, were that spider's brothers, sisters, cousins, aunts, and uncles, who were getting up to no good elsewhere. Angie's spider was big, but it was very much the runt of the litter.

And while Angie's husband was busy thwacking that one with a shoe, not too far away, its bigger, meaner relatives were preparing to come scurrying out of the shadows . . .

Your friend,
Hacker Murphy

CHAPTER TWO

HOLIDAY OF A LIFETIME

Jake Latchford sat squashed into the middle seat in the back of the car, his best mate, Liam, on one side, Liam's sister, Sarah, on the other. The journey was not going particularly well.

Hrrrrruuuuwwwwp!

Bleuuuuurrrkkggg!

Hnnnggggggrammaooooof!

'That's it, Liam, you get it out, sweetheart,' said Jake's mum, looking back at him over her shoulder and smiling kindly. It was alright for her, Jake thought. She and his dad were up front with the windows wide open. They didn't have to sit next to Liam as he hurled his stomach contents into a carrier bag for the tenth time in twenty minutes.

4

They'd stopped the first few times to let him throw up outside, but Dad had quickly come to the conclusion that if they didn't get moving soon, they'd never get to where they were going, so now Liam was reduced to chucking up into a series of supermarket carrier bags Jake's mum kept in the glovebox for just such an emergency.

Jake turned away and faced Sarah. They both had their jumpers over their mouths and noses to block out the smell. It wasn't working very well, though. Jake could only imagine what his poor dog, Max, was going through. He doubted Max would be enjoying having a vastly superior sense of smell today.

'Is he always like this on car journeys?' Jake asked.

Sarah shrugged. 'Depends. Sometimes he's fine. Other times, it's vomit central. The longer the journey, the worse he gets.'

Dad glanced in the rear-view mirror. 'We've only been driving for twenty minutes,' he pointed out. 'Thank God we're not going far.'

As the start of the October half-term holiday goes, it wasn't great. Jake had been excited when Dad announced that he'd won a holiday, and even more so when he said Liam and Sarah could come along, too. Jake had been hoping for Spain, or Tokyo—Florida, maybe. Instead, the trip was taking them all the way

5

from their home town of Larkspur-on-Sea to . . .

'Lower Larkspur,' Mum said, reading the town's *Welcome* sign as they drove past.

'Uh-uh,' said Dad, shaking his head. 'Lower Larkspur-*on-Sea*'. He tilted his face towards the open window and sniffed deeply. 'Smell that fresh sea air, kids?'

Sarah and Jake both shook their heads. Liam puked noisily into a 'bag for life'.

'No,' said Dad, smirking. 'Perhaps not, eh? Still, not far to go now, Liam!'

Liam managed a thumbs up before he buried his face in the bag and let rip again.

Yep, some holiday this was turning out to be. Still, it could only get better, Jake reckoned.

But he was wrong.

One of the few interesting things about Larkspur-on-Sea is that it isn't actually very close to the sea, at all. It's Larkspur-Quite-Near-But-Not-*That*-Near-The-Sea, if anything. Lower Larkspur-on-Sea was different in that it *was*, in fact, very close to the sea. Ironically, though, it was over fifteen miles from Larkspur, and the two towns were separated by three small villages and a river.

While it wasn't all that near Larkspur geographically, both towns were identical in one very important respect.

'Wow, this place is boring,' said Liam, as he, Jake, and Sarah wandered along a quaint little cobbled street. 'I almost miss throwing up. At least that was interesting.' He smiled fondly. 'It's amazing some of the colours that come out of you after your fifth or sixth really big heave.'

'Thanks for that,' said Sarah, wrinkling her nose.

'Some of it was green,' Liam continued.

'Yes, right, enough!' Sarah said, scowling at her brother. 'Don't want to know.'

They turned a corner at the end of the road and saw the beach spread out before them. Actually, calling it a 'beach' was being generous. There were no rolling dunes or soft, powdery sands. Instead, there were lots of damp, grey rocks all smeared with seaweed, and the coldest-looking water Jake had ever seen. Just the sight of it made him pull his jacket tighter around himself.

'Should we go for a swim?' Liam asked.

'What, in there?' said Jake. 'We'd freeze!'

Sarah shook her head. 'Nah. The polar bears would eat us first.'

Liam's jaw dropped in surprise. Sarah sighed. 'There aren't actually polar bears in the water,' she said. 'I was joking.'

Liam snapped his mouth shut. He frowned, looking a little annoyed. 'How many times have I told you, Sarah? Never joke about polar bears.'

'Uh, zero times,' said Sarah. 'You've literally never said that, ever.'

'Haven't I?' said Liam. 'What am I thinking of, then?'

'As usual, I have absolutely no idea,' said Sarah.

They strolled across the street and onto the promenade that ran for a mile or more along the shore. The closer they got to the water, the more overpowering became that 'fresh sea air' Jake's dad had mentioned. The stench was almost as bad as the one in the car had been, at the height of Liam's puke-fest.

Jake tucked his hands in his jacket pockets and gazed down at the slimy greenery coating the rocks. It reminded him of the weeds that had entangled him while canoeing on their school trip a few weeks earlier—or the slimy green algae the Creeper had used to infect the water supply back in . . .

No. He was on holiday. He wasn't going to think about the Creeper, or the terrible things he'd done to Jake and his friends. This was a chance to get away, relax, and have fun!

Jake looked along the empty seafront. Seagulls had torn open a bin bag and litter now flitted around over the rocks.

Yeah. Right. *Fun*.

'Should we go down there?' Liam asked.

'I can't imagine why we would want to,' said Sarah, shivering in the cold.

Liam puffed out his cheeks. 'If we go down there and see how awful it is, maybe this bit up here won't seem so bad.'

Jake attempted a smile. 'Come on, guys. This place isn't completely terrible.'

Liam and Sarah both nodded. 'You're right,' said Liam. 'It is mostly terrible, though.'

'Well, yeah, obviously it's mostly terrible,' agreed Jake. 'There's no denying it's *mostly* terrible. But they've got an arcade.'

'Which is currently closed,' said Liam.

'And a sweet shop.'

'Also not open yet,' Liam added.

Sarah elbowed her brother in the ribs and flashed Jake a smile. 'You're right. And the fact is, our parents are working all through the holidays, so if we hadn't come we'd be stuck at home,' she said.

'With games consoles and crisps,' said Liam. 'Lounging in bed until noon. Netflix available on demand . . .'

Sarah elbowed him again. Liam grinned at Jake. 'I mean, yeah, totally—thanks, mate. Really appreciate you inviting us along.'

Jake shook his head, but couldn't stop himself smiling. 'Come on, we haven't explored the cottage yet. Maybe it's better than it looked from the outside.'

'Yeah, maybe!' said Liam, with a little too much enthusiasm. 'But I doubt it!'

The old floorboards creaked beneath the hall carpet as Jake, Liam, and Sarah crept across it. There was no real reason for sneaking around, other than that it felt like the type of house where you shouldn't make too much noise, just in case you accidentally woke up the ghosts.

Liam had guessed the age of the house as 'a thousand years old' although had admitted, when pressed, that he was no expert in the matter. Jake reckoned he probably wasn't too far off, though. With its worn carpets, faded wallpaper, and woodworm-infested antique furniture, the whole place looked ancient.

It smelled ancient, too. A weird, stale sort of odour hung in the air like an unwanted guest. Or, as Liam put it, like a fart in a lift. It wasn't actually a farty sort of smell, though. It was more like dead flowers left to rot, and Jake found himself thinking about their encounters with the Creeper again.

He pushed the thought away and followed Liam and Sarah up the grand, but rickety staircase to check out the bedrooms. The stairs must once have been pretty grand and impressive, Jake thought, but now the carpet was threadbare, and every step creaked out the note of what sounded like a worryingly sinister tune.

'Check out this bloke,' said Liam, stopping at the top of the stairs. An enormous oil painting hung there, its frame thick with dust. It showed an older man with grey hair and the bushiest eyebrows Jake had ever seen. He was expensively dressed and seemed to sneer down his nose at the children as they stood looking up.

'He looks like a charmer,' said Sarah. She glanced

over at her brother before he could reply. 'I was being sarcastic.'

'Oh. Gotcha.' Liam bobbed his head left and right. 'His eyes seem to follow you, like the eyes in all them old paintings.'

'It *is* an old painting,' Jake pointed out.

Liam stopped bobbing. 'Oh, yeah. Good point. That'll be why then. Pretty creepy, though.' He shivered and looked around them. 'Do you reckon this place is haunted?'

Sarah snorted. 'Don't be ludicrous. There's no such thing as—'

A white shape jumped at them from the shadows, its arms flapping, an eerie moan floating around it.

'Ghost!' Liam yelped, but Jake caught him before he could run away.

'I don't think so,' Jake sighed. 'Very funny, Dad.'

Jake's dad pulled the sheet away to reveal his beaming grin. 'Gotcha!' he said. He gestured around. 'What do you think?'

'It's ... um ... interesting,' said Jake, as diplomatically as he could.

'What's the smell?' asked Sarah.

'Uh, I think that was me,' said Liam. 'Mr L gave me a fright.'

'No, not *that* smell,' Sarah sighed. 'The flowery one.'

Jake's dad shrugged. 'Lavender, I think. They put little bags of it in the bedroom drawers to keep insects away. They can't stand the stuff.'

'Them and me both,' said Liam. 'It reeks.'

'I've been meaning to ask, Dad,' said Jake, the floorboards creaking beneath his feet. 'Where exactly did you win this holiday, anyway?'

Dad frowned. 'I can't really remember. A magazine, I think.'

'Was it *Big Creepy Houses You'll Never Want to Visit Monthly*?' asked Liam.

'Haha,' said Dad. 'Yeah, something like that, probably. Speaking of creepy, though . . . ' He leaned in closer and whispered, 'Have you checked out the basement?'

Jake, Liam, and Sarah all gulped at once. 'There's a basement?' said Jake.

Dad nodded slowly. 'Of course there is, big old house like this. And do you know what's down there?'

Jake shook his head. 'No. What?'

Dad leaned back and smiled. 'No idea,' he said in his normal voice. 'How about you three pop down and have a look?'

A few minutes and several creaky floorboards later, the three friends stood at the top of a flight of steps leading down into a dark, shadowy basement below.

These steps were so ancient they made the rickety main staircase look like a shopping centre escalator by comparison.

The wood was warped and rotten in places, while the banister was nothing more than a thin plank that had been nailed to the wall. A faint breeze wafted up, making a soft whispering sound as it played across the steps.

There was a light switch just inside the door. That was the good news. The bad news was that it didn't appear to be connected to anything. It gave a dull *click* when Sarah flicked it, but the basement remained in darkness.

'Well, this has been lovely,' said Liam, rubbing his hands together. 'Now, who's for swimming? I'm sure the water's warmer than it looks.'

'You're not scared, are you?' said Sarah, looking at Liam and Jake in turn. The boys both shook their heads, shrugged, then nodded.

'A bit,' Jake admitted.

'Look at it!' said Liam. 'There could be anything down there. A monster. A snake. A *different* snake!'

'The Creeper,' said Jake, and all three fell silent for a while.

Eventually, Sarah gave herself a shake. 'Of course he isn't. There's nothing scary down there. It'll be fine.'

She saw the doubt on the boys' faces. 'Fine. I'll go first. But trust me, it's perfectly safe. There's nothing to worry about.'

Jake and Liam watched Sarah march down the stairs until she was swallowed by the dark. They waited for a moment, but she didn't come racing back up again.

'Huh,' said Jake. 'Maybe it *is* OK.'

And that was when the screaming started.

CHAPTER THREE

THE CREATURE IN THE DARKNESS

A crash followed the cry. Jake and Liam exchanged terrified looks, then hurried down the stairs into the basement. Scared or not, there was no way they were leaving Sarah to face whatever was down there alone. Besides, she'd never let them hear the end of it if they didn't at least try to help.

The screaming stopped almost as quickly as it had started, and by the time the boys reached the bottom of the stairs, the basement was completely silent.

'Sarah?' Liam whispered. 'Are you dead?'

'If she's dead, how can she answer you?' Jake asked.

'Good point,' whispered Liam. 'Sarah, if you're dead, knock once for "yes".'

'Of course I'm not dead,' said Sarah from the darkness. Her voice took Liam and Jake by surprise, and made them both yelp in fright.

'Oh yeah? Well, well . . . that's exactly what you would say if you *were* dead,' Liam pointed out.

Sarah switched on her mobile phone and the dim light pushed aside some of the darkness. 'If I was dead, could I do this?' she asked, then she punched Liam on the arm.

'Ow! OK, OK,' Liam conceded. 'Fine, you're not dead.'

'Why did you scream?' asked Jake.

Sarah stepped closer. She looked a little embarrassed. 'Well, the thing is, I was attacked by a—'

'Ghost!' yelped Liam, pointing past her.

Jake rolled his eyes. 'Not again, mate,' he began, then he froze when he saw a dark shape moving deeper into the basement. Now his eyes were adjusting to the gloom, Jake could see a little window right at the top of the basement wall, where it met the ceiling. The glass in the window had been painted over, but something was moving in front of it now. Something with bright green eyes that seemed to glow in the light from Sarah's phone.

It wasn't a ghost. It was the Creeper!

'Miaow,' said the Creeper.

17

Sarah shone the light from her screen towards it.

It wasn't the Creeper. It was a cat. Quite a big cat, but a cat, all the same. It was perched on the high windowsill, gazing down at them.

'You were attacked by a cat?' Jake asked Sarah.

She shifted uncomfortably. 'What? No,' she said. 'By a spider.'

Jake and Liam both stared at her for a moment, then began to snigger.

'How could a spider attack you?' Liam asked. 'Did it have a very small gun?'

'Shut up! It wasn't funny,' Sarah protested. 'It dropped off the ceiling and landed on my head!'

The boys' faces turned red as they held their laughter in.

'And then I fell into a rack of shelves and knocked over a load of old paint cans.'

That did it. Liam and Jake both exploded in fits of giggles. Sarah glared at them for several long seconds until they eventually stopped.

Jake cleared his throat. 'Ahem. Yes. Sorry about that.'

'I should think so!'

'Is it still in your hair?' Jake asked, standing on his tiptoes and examining the top of Sarah's head. She shuddered violently.

'It had better not be!' Sarah said. Jake was surprised to see her so shaken up. She was usually the coolest one in a crisis, and he'd always considered her the bravest of the bunch. To see her scared of a little spider was a bit weird.

Sarah pointed towards the corner. 'I think I flicked it over that way somewhere,' she said, shining the phone's light in that direction.

'Look out, it's behind you!' Liam bellowed. Sarah almost hit the roof, then she did actually hit Liam when she realized he was winding her up.

'Cut it out, Liam, it's not funny,' she warned him.

'It's a bit funny,' argued Liam.

'I think I see it,' said Jake.

'Don't you start!' Sarah snapped.

'No, really,' said Jake. He took Sarah's arm and guided the phone light over to the corner. A squat, fat, eight-legged bug lurked on the floor, angled in such a way it looked as if it might be staring straight at them.

'Wow. It is a big 'un, isn't it?' Jake said.

Sarah convulsed in horror and took a step back. 'Yuck,' she said. 'It's even worse than I thought. I can't believe that thing was on my head!'

It wasn't that the spider was *huge*, exactly. It wasn't a tarantula or a giant huntsman, or anything like that. It was just a normal, everyday house spider, albeit a particularly big one. Its long, slender legs tapered out from its black, egg-shaped body, and as it crept across the floor, Jake could almost have sworn he heard the faint pitter-patter of tiny footsteps.

'It's coming for you, Sarah. It's coming!' Liam cried. 'Run for your life!'

Sarah hit him again. It hurt quite a lot, and he decided it was probably time to stop doing that joke now.

'Squash it!' she yelped.

'That seems a bit harsh,' said Jake. 'I mean, it's not like it can hurt you.'

'What, you mean apart from jumping on my head and knocking me into a shelf full of paint tins?'

Sarah briefly flicked the phone's glow across to a broken rack of shelves. As well as paint tins, plastic squirty bottles, spray cans, and various cleaning supplies lay in a heap on the floor. She quickly turned the light back on the spider before it could sneak away somewhere then pounce on her again when she wasn't looking.

Too late!

Sarah swept the light across the floor, panicking. 'Where is it? Where did it go?'

Jake and Liam both looked around. 'Um, dunno,' Jake admitted. 'It was there a second ago.'

I know it was there a second ago.' Sarah snapped.
'But where is it *now?*'

'It's on your foot!' Liam yelped.

Sarah turned and glared at him. 'Will you stop doing that?' she said, slapping him on the upper arm.

'Ow!' said Liam. 'I'm not joking. It really is on your foot.'

His sister's eyes went wide. She looked down. Sure enough, the spider was crawling along her shoe, making a frantic dash for her leg.

Sarah made a noise. It wasn't a noise she had ever felt the need to make before. Looking back later, she'd admit it wasn't a noise she was particularly proud of, either. It was a sort of high-pitched '*Nyaaarroouumf!*' that rolled up from inside her and burst from her lips all by itself.

Her leg came up all by itself, too. It kicked out, trying to flick the spider away, but the arachnid held on. Sarah kicked again, and again, desperately trying to get the thing off before it could scramble up the leg of her jeans.

With a final furious foot flick, the spider lost its grip. It flipped end over end as it sailed through the air, and landed on the floor with a soft *paff*. Almost immediately, it began racing across the basement floor again.

And then, so suddenly it made all three children cry out in fright, the cat pounced down from the windowsill. It landed right behind the spider, its green eyes gazing down, its tongue flicking hungrily across its lips.

The spider stopped.

The spider looked up.

And then, with a snap of feline jaws, the spider was gone.

Or rather, most of it was gone. A couple of legs stuck out from the cat's mouth, flapping helplessly. Jake imagined the bug was angrily waving its fists at them. *'I'll get you next time, you pesky kids!'*

The legs were sucked in as the cat swallowed, then it let out a satisfied purr and hopped back up onto the windowsill.

A shocked silence followed. Liam was the first to break it. 'OK, well that's one of the worst things I've ever seen. Poor spider.'

'What do you mean, "poor spider"?' said Sarah. 'Poor me! That thing was out to get me.'

'I'm not sure it was,' said Jake.

'Well, you're wrong. It was,' said Sarah, crossing her arms to signal that the conversation was over. Wow. Jake had never seen her even close to this worked up before. It turned out she was more afraid of spiders than she was of the Creeper's evil plant monsters, or genetically engineered potato men. Who knew?

Jake shrugged. 'Well, give me a spider over *you know who* any day.'

Liam nodded. 'Hitler, you mean?'

'What? No!'

'Darth Vader?'

'No! The Creeper!'

'Oh, right, yeah,' said Liam. 'Him. Gotcha. That makes much more sense.'

There was a *thud* from the window that made everyone jump again. The cat had climbed outside and the window had flapped closed behind it. Jake could see the latch was broken, so the cat would just have to push from the other side to open it again, meaning it could come and go as it pleased.

'Where do you reckon the cat came from?' Liam asked.

Jake shrugged. 'One of the neighbours, probably. There's a church out the back. It might be a church cat.'

Liam frowned. 'What's a church cat?'

'A cat that lives in a church,' said Jake. 'The clue's in the name.'

'Oh, like a church mouse, you mean?' Liam asked.

'Well, kind of,' said Jake. 'Only sort of the exact

opposite.'

'I don't care where it came from, I'm just glad that it did,' said Sarah. She looked down at her shoe and shuddered at the memory of the spider sitting there. 'Now come on, let's go upstairs before anything else comes jumping out at us.'

With Sarah leading the way, they headed for the stairs. Jake hung back a moment to take one final look around the dark, shadowy basement. The cat was back at the window, its green eyes just visible through scratches in the painted pane. It stared at him, and its eyes seemed brighter somehow, and more piercing. Jake had a sudden urge not to be in the basement any more.

'Hey, wait for me,' he said, then he darted up the stairs, out into the hallway, and slammed the door behind him.

CHAPTER FOUR

THE GHOST OF LADY MASON

Jake, Liam, and Sarah spent the rest of the afternoon exploring the house, with Max trotting along behind them, wagging his tail. The whole place was pretty creepy, but nowhere near as bad as the basement.

The stuffed animal heads were a bit disturbing. One room in particular was full of them. All sorts of creatures stuck out from wooden mounts on the wall. There was a variety of deer, a wild boar, and some sort of goat which, understandably, looked quite annoyed. There was a fox head, too, something that looked like a raccoon, and even a duck. It was as though someone had desperately wanted to own a zoo, but only had room for little bits of each animal.

Six seconds after stepping into the room, the three

25

of them had stepped out again, and quietly agreed never to set foot in there again.

There were more paintings of the same scowling old man they'd seen earlier, as well as one or two showing a woman. She looked to be a few years younger than the man, and there was a sadness in her eyes which made her portraits quite hard to look at for any length of time without getting depressed.

Liam suggested drawing a moustache and glasses on her to make her look a bit more cheerful, but Jake reckoned they'd probably get into quite a lot of trouble for that, so they didn't bother.

There was something strangely familiar about the man, though. They all agreed they vaguely recognized him, but no-one could place where from.

There was a small library at the back of the house. Ancient leather-bound volumes lined the tall shelves, and a single armchair had been positioned in the corner, with a view out through the window.

The old church Jake had spotted on the drive in was just at the end of the back garden. Jake could see a few crumbling headstones in the church grounds. Great. Not only was this the spookiest house he'd ever been in, it also backed directly onto an old graveyard. As if he wasn't creeped out enough!

Every room they went in had that same strange smell. They'd looked in a few drawers and found little purple bags with dried flowers inside.

'Lavender,' Sarah confirmed. 'Like Jake's dad said.'

'How do you know that?' Liam snorted. 'Since when did you become an expert on flowers?'

'I'm not,' Sarah said. 'But I *am* an expert on reading.' She pointed to a handwritten label wrapped around the neck of the bag, sealing it closed. 'La-ven-der,' she said, slowly and deliberately. 'See?'

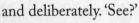

'And this stuff is supposed to keeps bugs away?' said Liam. He grinned at his sister. 'Want us to cover you in it in case any spiders come back?'

Sarah gave this some serious consideration, but decided that the smell would quickly become too much to deal with. 'I'll cope,' she said. 'I'll just avoid going into the basement again.'

'Or the attic,' said Jake.

'There's an attic?!' Sarah spluttered.

'Yeah,' said Jake. 'I think so.'

'That's bound to be *crawling* with spiders,' said Liam. 'I bet they're all backed up like a traffic jam around the hatch, just waiting to scuttle all over anyone who—'

'Right, yes, thank you, Liam!' Sarah yelped. 'Let's avoid the basement *and* the attic, in that case.' She shuddered violently and closed the drawer. 'Is there anywhere in this house that *isn't* all spooky and weird?'

The answer to that question turned out to be a pretty definitive, 'No.'

As they explored, the three friends found more paintings, more stuffed heads—and more dust than they'd even thought possible. Chandeliers swung and curtains twitched on unseen breezes. Floorboards creaked and groaned beneath their feet. And all the while, they couldn't shake the feeling that the fierce-looking old man in the paintings was watching their every move.

After a quick search upstairs, they found their bedrooms. Sarah's room must once have been lavishly decorated, but now it was as old and tired as the rest of the house. A four-poster bed stood at one end of the room, with an enormous oak wardrobe at the opposite end.

'What's in there, do you think?' Jake whispered. There was something ominous about the wardrobe that made him want to whisper.

'I don't know,' said Sarah. 'Narnia, maybe?'

'Or every single one of my childhood nightmares?' Liam guessed.

Cautiously, Jake approached the wardrobe doors. He gripped the handles for a moment, working up courage, then he pulled them both open. All three children screamed at the sight of the scary old man lurking inside.

It was Sarah who realized that it was just another painting of the same old guy they'd seen all around the house. He looked mean in every painting they'd seen so far, but in this one the expression on his face made him look practically demonic.

'There is definitely something familiar about that guy,' said Jake.

'Wait! I know!' said Liam. 'He's the bloke from the paintings.'

'Yeah, no, I meant . . .' Jake closed the wardrobe. 'Doesn't matter. Let's move on.'

Jake and Liam's room was right next door. To their delight, they didn't have a scary wardrobe that was possibly a portal to another dimension in their room. They didn't have very much of anything, in fact. Just an old wooden bunk-bed, which Liam immediately claimed the top bunk of, and a single bedside table with a cheap lamp sitting on it. Jake was just happy it was an electric lamp, and not some weird old gas thing he'd have to light with a match.

A floorboard squeaked behind them. Jake and Liam both gasped in shock and spun around. Sarah, who was pretty confident a spider hadn't made the noise, was less panicked. Max darted under the bed and hid there, his bum and back legs poking out and fully visible.

'Sorry, did I scare you?' asked Jake's mum.

Liam laughed far too loudly. 'Haha! What? No! Us? Pah! Who? Me and him? Never!' He swallowed and nodded. 'Little bit,' he admitted.

'Sorry about that,' said Mrs Latchford. 'I just came up to tell you your tea's ready. Jake's dad popped out to get us all fish and chips.'

'Yes!' cheered Liam and Jake together.

'But it was shut.'

'Oh.'

Mum grinned. 'Nah, just kidding. Come on, the food's all set out downstairs.'

At the mention of the word 'food,' Max shot out from under the bed and raced out of the room, his little tail wagging excitedly. The look on Liam's face suggested that if he'd had a tail, it would be wagging, too.

'Hey, Max, wait for me!' he cried. Jake and Sarah followed him out of the room, and the stink of lavender was replaced by a much nicer smell.

'Mmm,' they both said together. 'Chips!'

After they'd stuffed their faces on fish and chips, Jake, Liam, Sarah, and Jake's parents sat around the house's big dining table, eating little tubs of ice cream Mr Latchford had bought on the way back from the chip shop. Liam had kept one of his pickled onions aside, and it now sat on top of his ice cream like a big white cherry. Jake felt his stomach do a flip every time he looked at it.

'It's the contrast of textures that make this dish work,' said Liam, doing his best TV chef voice. 'The smooth, silky vanilla of the ice cream. The vinegary crunch of the onion.'

'The mind-boggling strangeness of my brother,' Sarah added, and everyone laughed.

'Yeah, bit weird, mate,' said Jake, licking a blob of ice cream from his little plastic spoon.

'You want to know what's really weird?' said Dad, leaning forwards in his chair as if about to share some big secret. He waited until he was sure he had everyone's attention. 'This place.'

'You can say that again,' said Jake.

'No, but really,' said Dad. 'I've been doing some reading about this house, and believe it or not, it turns out it's got a pretty spooky past.'

Jake, Liam, and Sarah glanced at the room around them. 'Yeah, I can absolutely believe that,' Jake replied.

'It was built back in the eighteenth century by a fella called Lord Mason. You might have seen one of his portraits.'

'Mean-looking old bloke?' Liam asked. 'Looks like he wants to bite your head off?'

'That's him. Well, it turns out he wasn't as mean as he looked.' Dad glanced left and right, as if making sure no one was listening, before speaking again. 'He

32

was even *worse*.'

Thunder rumbled. At least, that's what it sounded like. 'Sorry,' said Liam, thumping his chest. He burped again. 'It's the pickled onions.'

'What do you mean "worse"?' asked Sarah.

'Well, he was pretty much your stereotypical upper-class bully. Cruel to his servants, mean to the poor. He hated everyone, and everyone hated him right back. But it was Lady Mason who suffered the most.'

The children had all fallen silent now, waiting to hear what happened next.

'What did he do?' asked Jake's mum.

'He locked her up. Right here in this house,' said Dad. 'He kept her prisoner for years, never letting her see anyone. She went mad in the end.'

'Blimey,' whispered Liam.

Jake's dad glanced around the room. They'd switched off the overhead lights and lit the room with candles before they'd sat down to eat. It had seemed like a good idea at the time, but now the shadows scurried and crawled unpleasantly across the walls.

'She died right here in the house. Some say her ghost still

roams this place, and that—if you listen carefully—you can hear her desperate cries of despair drifting through the night.'

The silence in the room deepened as they all listened for the tormented howls of Lady Mason. Instead, they heard a squeaky *parp* as Max farted below the table.

'Yeah, but that's all nonsense, isn't it?' said Sarah. 'There's no such thing as ghosts.'

Dad raised an eyebrow. 'Oh . . . *isn't there*, Sarah? Isn't there?'

Sarah shook her head. 'No. There isn't.'

'No, fair enough, of course there isn't,' said Dad, grinning. 'Still, good story, isn't it?'

Mum finished off the last of her ice cream. 'And *this* is where you choose to take us on holiday. To the Crazy Lady Murder Mansion. Thanks for that.'

'I did say we should go to Disneyland,' Jake pointed out.

'But we didn't win a trip to Disneyland, did we?' said Dad.

'How *did* we win this trip?' asked Mum. 'And why on earth did you enter in the first place? I mean, what possessed you?'

Dad shrugged. 'Dunno. Can't remember. I actually thought you must've done it.'

Mum snorted. 'You thought *I* entered a competition

34

to come *here?*'

'I did think it was a bit strange,' Dad admitted. 'Still, we're here now. Just the five of us, Max . . . *and the ghost of Lady Mason!*'

He jumped up from the table and let out a ghostly scream. Jake rolled his eyes. Sarah smiled politely. Liam almost had a heart attack.

'Wah! Don't do that, Mr L!' he cried. 'I nearly brought my pickled onion back up!'

Another ghostly moan echoed around the room. 'Seriously, cut it out!' said Liam.

Dad frowned. 'That wasn't me.'

The sound came again. It was a low groaning noise that seemed to emerge from the walls all around them.

'It's her!' Liam yelped. 'It's Lady Ghostface, or whatever her name is!'

He jumped up from his chair and ran in tight, panicky circles. 'She's come for us! She'll kill us all! I'm too pretty to die!'

'Or it's the plumbing,' said Jake's mum. Liam stopped running in circles.

'What?'

'In old houses like these, the plumbing can make weird noises,' Mum said. She got up from her chair and crossed to the big, old-fashioned radiator standing against one wall. Bending down, she twisted a little tap where the radiator was attached to a long pipe. The ghostly noises stopped immediately.

'See?' said Mum. 'Nothing to worry about.'

Liam gulped. 'Unless it's the radiator that's haunted,' he whispered. 'And you've just set the ghost free!'

Mum smiled. 'I'll take my chances,' she said. She began to stack up the empty fish and chip boxes. 'Now, who's going to help me tidy up?' she asked, but by the time she'd finished the sentence, Jake, Liam, and Sarah had gone.

The three friends darted up the stairs, hoping the creaking of the steps wouldn't give them away. 'Phew, that was close,' Liam whispered.

'I know!' said Jake. 'We almost got roped into tidying up.'

'No, not that,' said Liam. 'I meant the ghost.'

Sarah tutted. 'Don't be stupid. There *is* no ghost.'

'How do you know?'

'Well, one, because there's no such thing as ghosts,' said Sarah. 'And two . . . Actually, I don't need a two. Point one pretty much covers it. Ghosts don't exist.'

'Oh yeah?' Liam snapped. 'Well . . . neither do spiders!'

Sarah and Jake both just stared at him until he spoke again.

'I mean, yes, obviously spiders exist,' he admitted.

'I just mean it's stupid to be scared of them. Unlike ghosts.'

They creaked and squeaked along the landing until they reached Sarah's room. 'I'm going for an early night,' said Sarah, yawning. 'I want to catch up on some reading.'

'Boring!' said Liam. 'We're going to stay up until four in the morning doing fun stuff, aren't we, Jake?'

'Yeah!' said Jake. He thought for a moment. 'What sort of fun stuff?'

Liam opened his mouth, then frowned. 'Well we could . . . ' He puffed out his cheeks. 'Did you bring your Xbox?'

'No.'

'Right,' said Liam. 'Any board games?'

'I think I saw an old Monopoly board downstairs,' Jake replied.

Liam shuddered. 'Right. An early night it is, then!'

'Probably for the best,' agreed Jake. 'We've got lots of fun planned for tomorrow.'

'Have we?' said Sarah, surprised.

Jake shook his head. 'No, not really. We could look at some seaweed again for a bit. Maybe the arcade will be open.'

Sarah smiled. 'Wow. And to think, you wanted to go to Disneyland.'

They all said goodnight, then Jake and Liam headed next door to their room. It looked even more grim than either of them remembered.

'Still want the top bunk?' Jake asked.

Liam nodded. 'Yeah. That way, if any ghosts or flesh-eating ghouls do come in, they'll have to get through you first.'

'Thanks for that,' Jake muttered.

'Oh, and one other thing,' said Liam. He clicked the switch on the bedside lamp and it flickered into life. 'We are *definitely* leaving the light on.'

CHAPTER FIVE

THE THING IN THE GRAVEYARD

Next morning, a bleary-eyed Jake plodded down the stairs, yawning and scratching his head. Liam had kept waking him up, demanding to know what various noises he'd either heard or imagined had been.

The first few times it had happened, Jake had tried to reassure his friend that it wasn't the malevolent spirit of Lady Mason come to get him from beyond the grave, and had explained the noises were the wind, the house's old wood creaking in the draught, and his dad snoring, in that order.

After being woken up for the sixth or seventh time, Jake had resorted to burying his head under his pillow and ignoring Liam. This only made Liam panic more, though, and Jake had opened his eyes more than once to find him leaning down from the top bunk, staring at him in wide-eyed terror.

'Hey Mum. Hey Dad,' he said, shuffling into the kitchen. He opened the fridge and took out a carton of milk, and was halfway through pouring himself some cereal when he realized there was no one else in the kitchen.

A note lay on the kitchen table, written in Mum's studious handwriting:

Gone for a walk.
Back later.

There was a sudden thunder of footsteps from the hall outside. Jake crossed to the door just as Liam came charging through. His eyes were wide and his hair was standing on end. 'You left me!' Liam said. 'You just left me alone in there!'

'You were asleep,' Jake pointed out.

'That's even worse!' said Liam. 'Anything could have got me when I was sleeping. You should have been there to protect me.'

'Boo!'

Liam almost hit the roof as Sarah jumped into the

kitchen. Unlike the boys, who were both still in their pyjamas, she was fully dressed and looked ready to go out.

'Hurry up and eat something,' she urged. 'I've been thinking about the ghost.'

'I *knew it!*' cried Liam. 'They *are* real!'

Sarah tutted and rolled her eyes. 'Of course they aren't. But I got thinking about the story of Lord and Lady Mason. They were real. They might be buried in that graveyard out the back. I thought we could take a look.'

Liam's jaw flopped open. 'Why? What possible reason would we have for going and digging up a couple of old graves?!'

'We're not going to dig them up,' Jake said. He shot Sarah a sideways glance. 'We aren't, are we?'

'Of course not,' said Sarah. 'I just thought it'd be interesting to see if they're buried there. Since we're here, we might as well try and find out some of the local history.'

Liam frowned. 'Or, because, you know, that sounds like the most boring thing in the whole world, we could go to the arcade, where there are no dead people.'

'Come on, it'll only take a little while to check out the headstones, then we can go to the arcade later. It won't be open yet, anyway,' Sarah pointed out.

Jake shrugged. 'Yeah, fair enough. I mean, it's only a graveyard. What's the worst that could . . . ?'

He caught Liam's expression. 'Yeah,' Jake said, thinking back over all the terrible things that had happened to them lately. 'Probably best not to tempt fate.'

Liam groaned. 'Ugh. Can I just stay here?'

'On your own, you mean?' said Jake.

Sarah smirked. 'Oh no, he won't be on his own,' Sarah said. 'He'll be here with the ghost.'

Liam's face turned ash-grey. 'On s-second thoughts,' he stammered. 'Last one there's a rotten egg.'

Jake and Sarah both watched as Liam raced for the door, pulled it open, then ran outside. 'At what point, do you think, will he realize he's still wearing his pyjamas?' Sarah asked.

From outside, there came a short, sharp, 'Yikes!'

'Ooh,' said Jake, finishing pouring his cereal. 'I'd say roughly around now.'

Twenty minutes later, a fully-dressed Liam skulked along behind Jake and Sarah as they strolled through the graveyard.

The headstones were ancient, with most of the lettering faded by age and the weather. By the looks of it, no one had been buried here for well over a hundred years, so either there was another graveyard in town, or the people in Lower Larkspur-on-Sea had all become *very* healthy over the past century.

The grass in the cemetery was straggly and overgrown, and nobody had laid flowers on any of the graves. Mind you, that wasn't a surprise. Some of these people were so old even their great-grandchildren were probably long dead.

'Look at this one. It's from 1735,' said Sarah, stopping at a particularly worn and weather-beaten headstone. It must once have been grand and ornately carved, but now most of the detail had been smoothed by centuries of wind and rain, and the writing was hard to make out.

Jake squatted down to study it. He traced his fingers across the carved letters, trying to make them out. 'Ernest . . . Heviot, I think,' he said.

Liam gasped. 'Not *the* Ernest Heviot?!'

Jake looked up. 'You've heard of him?'

'No, of course I haven't!' said Liam. 'You know what I *have* heard of, though? The arcade. And it sounds brilliant.' He pulled his jacket around himself. 'Better than hanging around here, anyway.'

'Relax,' Sarah told him. 'There are no ghosts. All the bodies are buried deep underground beneath tonnes of soil. Between that and, you know, being dead, they can't hurt you.'

She said it all in a sort of sneering tone that Liam didn't really like. He pointed to the headstone behind her. 'Spider.'

Sarah jumped and let out a loud, 'Eek!'

'Oh no,' said Liam, innocently. 'False alarm.'

Jake stood up and looked around at the other graves. 'Well, I don't see any Lord or Lady Mason here,' he said. 'But then I'm not really surprised. My dad was probably making it up. He loves telling ghost stories.'

'Well, I don't love hearing them,' said Liam. 'Can we go to the arcade now?'

Sarah sighed. 'I told you, it's not open yet!' She set off along the row of graves. 'Now come on, I want to take another look. I think there are some more headstones up this way.'

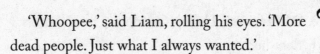

'Whoopee,' said Liam, rolling his eyes. 'More dead people. Just what I always wanted.'

The three friends didn't see a soul—living or dead—as they wandered through the graveyard. The long grass and weeds tangled around their feet, and Liam kept freaking out and screaming that one of the occupants of the graves had grabbed his foot.

They found a few other graves from the 1700s, when Lord and Lady Mason would have been knocking around the place, but their headstones weren't among them. Ernest Heviot was the earliest, back in 1735, and it was a good ten years or so until the next recorded death date.

'So, that means that Ernest would have been the first person buried here,' said Sarah. She looked around at the rows and rows of crumbling memorials and shuddered as a cool breeze swirled around her.

'Imagine that,' said Liam. 'Being here all on your own for ten years with no one around you.'

'Oh yeah, I bet he loved it when the neighbours moved in,' said Jake, smirking. 'Finally, someone to talk to!'

For a moment, Liam looked annoyed, as if Jake were making fun of him, but then he joined in with the joke. 'Good afternoon, Mr Heviot. I was hoping I could borrow a cup of sugar,' he said in a haughty voice. 'Mr Heviot? Hello? Goodness, he doesn't say much, does he?'

'And why is he so thin?' added Jake in a similar voice.

'And what on *earth* is that smell?' demanded Liam. The boys both laughed. Sarah smiled and rolled her eyes.

'Yeah, I'm sure that's exactly what it was like,' she said.

They wandered back towards the entrance, taking a long path that ran all the way to the back of the cemetery, then curved around the outside. Liam was complaining less now. He'd found a fun way to pass the time, and it was rapidly becoming his new favourite game. He hadn't worked out all the rules yet, but his working title for it was *Death Top Trumps*.

'Ooh, this one had leprosy,' he said, reading a gravestone. 'That's got to be, what? An eight out of ten?' His eyes lit up when he saw the next headstone. 'Dysentery! This poor fella literally pooped himself to death! Nine out of ten.'

'What's the actual scoring criteria you're working by?' asked Sarah. 'How is dysentery one better than leprosy?'

'*Kicked by a horse!*' Liam squealed, bouncing up and down in front of another headstone. 'This one was

46

killed by a kicking horse!'

'You do realize you're literally jumping for joy on that man's grave, yes?' said Jake.

Liam looked down, stopped jumping, then quickly side-stepped onto a path. 'Sorry, mate,' he said, raising his voice a bit, as if the two-hundred-year-old dead guy would be able to hear him. 'And bad luck with the whole horse thing.'

He fell into step alongside Jake and Sarah. 'Ten out of ten,' he whispered. 'We have a winner.'

Jake stopped so abruptly it took the others a few seconds to notice. They stopped, too, and turned back. 'What's up?' Sarah asked.

'Check that out,' said Jake. He was staring off to the right, away from the path and back towards the edge of the cemetery where it met a shadowy forest. A man stood there, his back to them. He seemed to be stroking a large hedge that stood on its own at the graveyard's edge.

The hedge was about the size of a large van, but there was something about the shape of it that had caught Jake's eye. The edges were formed into a series of regular points, and the way the leaves had grown created a pretty striking 3D effect. From this angle, the whole thing looked like—

'A spider's web!' Sarah gasped. She looked at the

47

boys. 'It does, right? It looks like a spider's web.'

Liam tilted his head left and right. 'You think? Nah, I don't see it,' he said. He clicked his fingers. 'I know. It looks like that old dinner lady who retired last year. Remember? The one with the ears.'

'They've all got ears,' said Jake.

'No, but this one had *ears*,' said Liam, cupping his hands at the side of his head. 'Like that elephant in *Dumbo*. Can't remember his name.'

'*Dumbo*,' said Sarah, and Jake wasn't sure if she was giving her brother the answer or insulting him. He decided not to ask.

'Excuse me?' called Liam, cupping his hands around his mouth and shouting. The gardener turned, but his face was hidden by the shadows of the bush. Liam pointed to the foliage. 'Is that the woman who used to work in our canteen?'

The man glared at them. He had a set of gardening shears held in front of him, held like a deadly weapon, the sharp blades pointed in Jake's direction.

Jake couldn't put his finger on it, but there was something about the gardener that made his skin crawl. He shuffled sideways and the tips of the shears turned to follow him.

It was then that Jake noticed the grass. Everywhere else in the cemetery, it was long and overgrown, but a circle directly around the man's feet looked like it had been neatly trimmed. As the gardener took a step forward, the long grass in front of him wriggled like a nest of snakes, and retreated into the ground, clearing a path for him.

Jake's breath caught in his throat. His stomach flipped.

No.

No, it couldn't be.

But it was. He knew it. The way he'd made Jake's skin crawl should have been enough of a warning. There was no doubt about it. This was the—

'Ghost!' cried Liam, pointing past the man into the woods.

This time, even Sarah let out a little yelp of fright. A dark, sinister shape was floating in the woods behind the gardener, hovering a half a metre off the ground.

'Run!' Liam cried. He was already halfway along the path and accelerating rapidly.

Sarah gulped. 'Well,' she whispered. 'Maybe just this once.'

With a final glance at the shape in the trees, she set off at a sprint, with Jake racing along beside her.

CHAPTER SIX

THE SUPPLY RUN

Jake and Sarah ran onto the street their holiday house was on and stopped by the front gate. There was no sign of Liam anywhere. Jake stood on the bottom railing of the gate to give himself a better view along the street in both directions.

'Can you see him?' Sarah asked, puffing slightly from the effort of running so far.

Jake shook his head and stepped down. 'No. No sign of him.'

'Psst.'

Jake froze. 'What was that?'

'Psst. Down here.'

Jake and Sarah both looked around for a moment, searching for the source of the voice. They eventually found Liam lying flat on his back beneath Jake's parents' car. 'Told you,' he said.

'Told us what?' asked Sarah.

'Ghosts, innit?' said Liam. 'They are real. Did it follow you?'

Jake looked back over his shoulder, suddenly terrified he'd see a monstrous shape behind him. The street was empty, and as silent as the grave.

'No. Come out.'

There was a scuffling sound from beneath the car that lasted for several seconds. 'Can't,' said Liam. An arm flopped out onto the ground. 'You'll have to pull.'

It took almost a minute of heaving to haul Liam out from beneath the car. When he stood up, his face was black with oil smears. 'I think your car's leaking,' Liam said.

'You don't say,' Sarah said.

'I think that's the least of our problems right now,' said Jake.

Liam nodded and they all headed for the front gate. 'Tell me about it,' he said. He tapped a finger to his ear and leaned closer to his sister. 'Sorry, Sarah, what was that?'

Sarah frowned. 'I didn't say anything.'

'Oh, didn't you? I thought I heard you apologize,' said Liam. 'I thought I heard you say, "You were totally right, Liam. Ghosts *do* exist. I'm so lucky to have such a wise and intelligent brother to help keep me right about such things." Did you say that?'

'No.'

'Sure?'

'Yes, I'm sure!' Sarah said. 'Whatever we saw in the woods, it wasn't a ghost. It couldn't have been. It was probably just . . . a person.'

'Yeah, you're right,' said Liam. 'Probably just a regular, everyday person floating fifty centimetres off the ground beside a creepy graveyard. Nothing spooky about that at all.'

'How do you know it was floating?' Sarah asked.

'Well, because it wasn't touching the ground,' Liam retorted. 'That was my first clue.'

'It *did* look like it was floating,' Jake admitted. 'But forget the ghost . . .' He shot Sarah a sideways glance. 'Or, you know, whatever it was. That's not our big problem. Our big problem is the—'

'Cat!' cried Liam.

Jake sighed. 'Seriously, will you *please* stop interrupting me like that?'

The cat from the basement sat in the middle of the path, its tail flicking lazily from side to side. In the light of day, it was a dirty, mangy-looking thing, with thin patches in its black fur which showed its skin below. One of its ears looked like it had got too close to a number of power tools, and half its whiskers were missing.

As the children approached, the cat stared at them, unblinking.

'Here, puss, puss,' said Sarah.

'Don't call it over!' Liam warned her. 'That thing's probably why everyone caught leprosy. Look at it!'

The cat didn't come closer. Its eyes flitted from Sarah to Jake to Liam in turn, its tail still tick-tocking left and right.

Even when they walked along the path towards it, the cat didn't budge. Instead, they were forced to step onto the grass and go round the animal to get to the cottage's front door. When they looked back, it had turned all the way around and was watching them again, its green eyes still not blinking.

'Do you think it lost its witch?' Liam asked.

Once they were inside, Jake charged through to the library, with its view of the graveyard. There was no sign of any ghosts hanging around out there, and

the gardener had vanished, too. The bush he'd been working on wasn't visible from this angle, though, so for all Jake knew he was still up there, stroking the thing's leaves.

'I'm still waiting for your apology,' said Liam, as he and Sarah entered the room. 'I know, you're so used to being right all the time it must be hard for you to admit you're wrong.'

'I'm not wrong,' said Sarah, sighing. 'Ghosts don't exist, therefore what we saw couldn't possibly have been a ghost.'

'So, what? It was just a regular floating woman then, was it?' Liam asked.

'Who says it was a woman?'

'I do,' said Liam. 'It was clearly a woman.'

Sarah shook her head. 'It was completely in shadow. It could have been a woman, a man, a big monkey in a suit . . .'

Liam's face lit up in delight.

'It wasn't a big monkey in a suit,' said Sarah.

Liam's face fell. 'Oh. That would've been amazing!'

'I want to go back,' Sarah announced. Now that her initial fright had passed, she was beginning to feel a bit stupid for running away the way she did. 'There'll be some evidence we can find. Footprints or something that will prove it wasn't a ghost.'

Jake turned from the window. 'Guys, we've got a bigger problem right now. Whatever was in the woods, it can wait.' He drew in a deep breath and glanced at Liam to make sure he wasn't going to interrupt before he could finish the next sentence.

'The gardener,' said Jake. 'I think . . . No, I *know*. I'm right, I'm sure of it.'

Sarah raised an eyebrow. 'Right about what?'

'It was the Creeper.'

Silence fell over the library as Sarah took in this new information.

'You really think the Creeper's here?' asked Sarah.

Liam cried out in fright and spun on the spot, his hands raised in a karate pose. 'Argh! Where?'

'Not literally here in this room,' said Sarah.

'The gardener,' explained Jake.

Sarah shook her head. 'I don't know, Jake . . .'

'Look, I know I got a bit . . . paranoid about the Creeper before,' Jake admitted.

'You mean you thought you saw him everywhere you looked?' Sarah said.

'Yeah,' said Jake, shifting uncomfortably on the spot. 'But this is different.'

'How?' asked Sarah. 'I mean, think about it. He had a set of gardening shears.'

'Which he pointed right at me,' Jake reminded her.

'I'm not saying he didn't react a bit oddly when he saw us,' said Sarah. 'But why would the Creeper have something designed for cutting up plants? He always says he's going to take revenge on people who do that.'

Jake shrugged. 'Maybe he doesn't stick to his own rules. Although, we never actually saw him using the shears, did we?'

Liam gasped. 'Maybe he wants to use them on us!' His eyes widened. 'He's going to chop all our fingers off. I bet you *anything*. I don't want to lose all my fingers! How will I scratch myself, or pick my nose?' He steadied himself against a bookshelf. 'I'll never play the piano again.'

Sarah tutted. 'You don't play the piano now.'

'Oh yeah,' said Liam, appearing to relax. He shrugged. 'Fair enough, then.'

'It was him,' Jake insisted. 'The grass moved around his feet. Tell me you saw that.'

Liam held up both hands in a weighing motion. 'Terrifying ghostly figure in the forest,' he said, moving one hand up and down. He turned his attention to the other hand. 'Some grass. Guess which one I was looking at.'

Jake tutted, then turned back to the window. He stood on his tiptoes, trying to see over the little hill to where they'd encountered the gardener. It was him, he could feel it. The Creeper was in Lower Larkspur-on-Sea.

'Why would he be here?' asked Sarah, as if reading his mind.

'Maybe he wants to check out the arcade. I hear it's brilliant,' said Liam, hoping someone took the hint. They didn't.

Jake shrugged, but didn't turn away from the window. 'This is the guy who made an army out of potatoes,' he reminded them. 'Since when did he make sense?'

'OK, fair point,' Sarah conceded. 'But I still think you're being paranoid again.'

Jake stopped trying to see over the crest of the hill. It was impossible from here. There was only one way they could investigate further.

'Let's go back,' he said, turning.

'Home?' said Liam. He clapped his hands, then rubbed them together. 'Now you're talking. This place is rubbish.'

'No, not home. Back out there,' said Jake, gesturing out at the graveyard. 'We need to know if that was the Creeper.'

Liam winced. 'Do we?'

'Well, I do,' said Jake.

'And I want to check out your ghost,' added Sarah.

Liam groaned. 'Fine. Let's all go out and get our fingers chopped off,' he said. 'But on one condition. If I'm going to die, I'm going out on a sugar high.'

He pointed dramatically to the door. 'To the sweet shop!'

Even the sweet shop turned out to be a bit disappointing—largely, as far as Liam was concerned, because it wasn't actually a sweet shop at all.

'I'm just saying, yes, they've got sweets, and I

applaud them for that,' Liam said, as he, Jake, and Sarah browsed the rows of chocolate bars and jars of hard candy. 'But it's not a sweet shop. It's a shop that sells sweets.'

Sarah shrugged. 'What's the difference?'

Liam snorted. 'Oh, you dear, foolish child,' he said. 'A sweet shop, right, sells sweets.'

'This place sells sweets,' said Jake.

'I wasn't finished,' Liam replied. 'A sweet shop sells sweets *and nothing else*.' He thought about this for a moment. 'Well, maybe ice cream.'

'And soft drinks,' said Jake.

'OK, sweets, ice cream, and soft drinks,' said Liam.

'Popcorn?' asked Sarah.

Liam sighed. 'OK, yes. Sweet shops sell sweets, ice cream, soft drinks, and popcorn. And maybe crisps, at a push. But nothing else.'

He strolled over to a display of household products. 'They don't, for example, sell toilet roll and bin bags.'

He gestured to a nearby shelf. 'Is that candy-coated baby powder?' he asked. 'Are those nappies chocolate flavoured? I don't think so.'

Jake shrugged. 'So? They've got sweets. What are you having?'

'Don't get me wrong, this is an excellent *corner* shop,' said Liam, returning to his friend's side. 'On my corner shop scale, it's a comfortable eight out of ten. But it isn't a sweet shop. Not by a long shot.'

Jake shot Liam a sideways look. 'You have a corner shop scale?'

'He does,' Sarah groaned. 'Don't get him started on it.'

'It's *very* detailed,' said Liam. Quite proudly, Jake thought.

Jake and Sarah both picked up a couple of chocolate bars each, then waited as Liam spent the next few minutes filling bags with candy teeth, gobstoppers, strawberry laces, and other assorted goodies.

Once he'd filled six separate bags, he picked up one of each chocolate bar on the top rack, and carried the whole lot in his arms like a newborn baby. 'Right,' he said. 'This'll do for now.'

When they reached the checkout, an old woman was already being served. They lined up behind her, waiting patiently while she and the middle-aged man behind the counter finished their conversation.

'Sorry, dear, we're all out of insect repellent,' the shopkeeper said. 'We've had a real run on it lately. Everyone's been buying the stuff.'

Liam turned to the others and raised his eyebrows. 'Insect repellent,' he whispered. 'In a so-called "sweet shop". I rest my case.'

'It'll be because of the spiders,' said the woman, and Sarah tensed so suddenly she squashed her Mars Bar. 'They've been bad these last few days. I found three in my bath just this morning.'

'There were a couple in here earlier, too,' said the shopkeeper, and Sarah's eyes shot to the floor. 'Tell you what, I'll put you some aside when the next delivery comes in, OK?'

'Ta, love,' said the old woman. She gave the man a wave, then shuffled off. 'Ta-ra!'

The shopkeeper smiled and looked at the children expectantly. Sarah had frozen to the spot. When Liam prodded her in the back she almost hit the roof.

'You OK, pet?' the shopkeeper asked.

'She doesn't like spiders,' Jake explained.

'One wrestled her to the ground yesterday,' added Liam.

Sarah shot him daggers, then deposited her partially-squashed chocolate bars on the counter. 'Just these, please.'

The man took the bars and scanned them.

'And all these,' said Liam, dumping his own haul onto the counter beside Sarah's. He smiled hopefully at his sister. 'I don't have quite enough money.'

Sarah tutted. 'Well, how much do you have?'

61

Liam's lips moved silently. He counted on his fingers. 'None,' he said, then he quickly changed the subject before Sarah could argue. 'Here, mate. Have you ever seen any ghosts around here?'

The shopkeeper raised his eyebrows in surprise as he set about scanning Liam's sweets. 'Ghosts? Not that I know of,' he said. 'I mean, Mrs Jasper, who was just in—she can look a bit ghostly without her make-up on, I suppose, but that's about it. Why do you ask?'

'Oh, no reason,' said Liam. He grabbed all his items from the counter, and flashed a grin at Sarah. 'Thanks, sis,' he said, then he turned on his heels and darted out of the shop before Sarah could stop him.

The shopkeeper smiled at her. 'Brothers, eh?'

Sarah sighed as she reached into her pocket for money. 'Seriously, you have *no* idea.'

CHAPTER SEVEN

WALL OF WEBS

By the time they'd walked back from the shop, Liam had eaten all his sweets and was hungrily eyeing up Sarah's.

'How are you not morbidly obese?' Sarah wondered.

Liam shrugged. 'I have a very active brain,' he said. 'It burns a lot of calories. The more I feed it, the smarter I get.'

Jake laughed. Liam glared at him, pretending to be offended. 'What are you laughing at? That's just science. Look, give me your Twix and I'll show you how much smarter I get.'

'Nah, you're alright,' said Jake.

The plan had just been to head straight to the graveyard, but as they were passing the house, Max came bounding along the path, yipping and barking excitedly.

'Ah, there you are!' called Dad from the doorway. He beckoned them inside. 'We've made lunch. I hope you're hungry.'

Liam's stomach rumbled. 'Perfect timing, Mr L,' he said. 'I am absolutely famished!'

Jake and Sarah watched Liam strut along the path and into the house. Sarah shook her head. 'Seriously, one of these days I swear he's going to explode.'

'How was your walk?' asked Jake, reaching across the table and helping himself to another sandwich.

They were eating lunch at the much smaller kitchen table, having decided the dining room was a little too grand—and far too creepy—to eat sandwiches and sausage rolls in.

'It was . . . nice,' said Dad.

'By which he means "awful",' Mum clarified.

'I wouldn't go that far,' said Dad. He caught his wife's expression. 'No, you're right, it was awful.'

'I think this sea air's going to poor Maxy's stomach,' Mum said, picking up the dog and cuddling him tightly. 'We had to stop every few minutes for him to *do his business*,' she added, whispering the last three words as if it was top secret classified information.

'By which she means, to do a big poo,' explained Dad, in what was a bit of an unnecessary detail during lunch, Jake thought. 'See anything weird?' Liam asked. 'Like, I don't know . . .'

'Don't say it,' Sarah warned.

'A *ghost*?'

Dad grinned. 'You mean like Lady Mason? No, she just haunts the house.'

'You'd think she'd go outside, wouldn't you?' said Jake, munching thoughtfully on a tiny sausage. 'I mean, if I'd been locked up in this place for years, then suddenly discovered I could walk through walls, I'd be off like a shot.'

'Where would you go?' said Dad.

'It's funny you should ask,' said Jake. 'Disneyland.'

Dad smiled. 'Ooh. Nicely played.'

'Thanks,' said Jake. He grabbed another sausage and stood up. 'We're going to head outside for a bit.'

'OK, but take Max with you,' said Mum, setting the dog down on the floor. 'He never did finish that poo.'

Jake kept low and dashed over to the next headstone. It was a big, ornate slab of granite with a cross etched into the stone. He ducked behind it, peered over the top, then gestured for Liam and Sarah to join him. They both scampered, low down, just like Jake had. Max trotted along behind them, his tail wagging happily. He had no idea what game they were playing, but it looked like fun.

'Any sign?' whispered Liam, taking cover behind the headstone.

'Nothing yet,' said Jake. They all knelt on the grass, then peeped over the top of the granite slab. They could just make out the weirdly-shaped bush, but there was no sign of the gardener or the shadowy shape in the woods.

'I think it's all clear,' said Sarah. 'I can't see anyone there.'

'Ghosts can turn invisible,' Liam pointed out.

'Or they could, if they existed,' Sarah corrected. 'But they don't.'

Jake decided to take a risk, and stood up. He stepped onto the path, and immediately felt a little less panicked.

If the plant-controlling Creeper really was here, then solid stone was a safer place to be standing than long grass.

Still, he braced himself for the monster to come lunging at him from somewhere. But the only sounds in the graveyard were the distant tweeting of birds and the soft rustling of the breeze through the grass.

Even Max looked relaxed and happy. If there had been danger nearby, Max would have reacted quickly. Probably by running away and hiding under Jake's bed, but there would have been some sort of reaction, at least. As it was, he scampered along at Jake's heel as they headed up the path towards the weird bush.

From this angle, he could see what Sarah was getting at. It did sort of look like a spider's web. He couldn't, however, see any resemblance to any school dinner ladies, past or present. Nor could he see any markings on the bush that suggested it had been cut into a web-like design. This, it seemed, was just its normal shape.

The gardener—or Creeper, if it really was him—was nowhere to be seen. The grass around the bush, which had looked short and neatly trimmed earlier, was long and unkempt, just like everywhere else in the cemetery.

There didn't seem to be anything more of interest

near the bush, so the friends turned their attention to
the forest. A wispy white fog was hanging around it,
making the trees difficult to see. At least, Jake thought
it was a fog. As he got closer, though, he realized his
first impression had been wrong.

Thousands of spiders' webs clung to the leaves and
branches, and dangled down like net curtains. Jake
heard Sarah gasp behind him, and guessed she had
figured out what the mist really was, too.

'You have got to be kidding me,' she said,
shuddering. 'Those can't all be webs.'

Liam stepped past Jake and approached the wispy
white wall. There were so many webs they'd all joined
together to form one big one. Liam reached out to
touch it, then stopped when Sarah hissed in fright.

'Liam! Stop! What are you doing?'

Liam looked back over his shoulder. 'Relax. It's just
some webs.'

'Hundreds of webs. *Thousands*,' Sarah corrected.

Liam shrugged. 'So? I'm not scared of a few
spiders.'

'A *few*?' Sarah yelped. She pointed to the web-wall.
'I didn't see any of those a couple of hours ago,' she
said. 'How many spiders do you think it would take to
make all that in one morning?'

Liam puffed out his cheeks. 'Twelve?'

'*Twelve*?!'

'Well, I don't know, do I?' Liam replied. 'I'm not an expert.'

'Really? You surprise me,' said Sarah.

'She might be right,' said Jake. He looked the mass of webbing up and down. There really was an awful lot of the stuff. 'Probably best not to touch it.'

Liam shrugged. 'Fair enough,' he said, turning. But as he did so his foot snagged on a tangle of weeds and he fell backwards, straight into the web.

For a moment, it looked as if the spider silk was going to be strong enough to hold him up, but then it snapped with an audible *twang* and Liam toppled like a falling tree into the forest.

All three held their breath as they waited to see what would happen next. Max, meanwhile, quietly finished his poo behind the bush.

To everyone's relief—especially Sarah's—an army of spiders didn't come swarming out across the webs to see what was for dinner. Liam picked himself up and dusted some of the cobwebs off him. The hole he'd made acted like a door, allowing Jake to step through after him. Sarah hung back, refusing to get any closer to the webbing.

Jake turned and looked back at the cemetery. This had to be around the spot where they'd seen the

69

ghostly figure, but there was no one around now.

'See anything?' Sarah called.

'Ghost-wise, you mean?' Jake called back. 'No, nothing.'

'Check for footprints.'

'There's some!' said Liam, pointing to a patch of mud behind him.

'Those are yours,' Jake said. He squatted down roughly at the spot they'd seen the shape, but there was nothing to suggest anyone had ever stood there. It looked like whatever they'd seen had been floating, after all.

As Jake stood up, something brushed against his head. He jumped back, startled, then stopped when he realized it wasn't a Creeper-controlled plant vine or a ghost. It was a long strand of spider silk, hanging down from a high branch. It was several times thicker than any web he'd ever seen and must've taken the spider hours to spin. It almost looked like a thick piece of string made from hundreds of thinner strands, all twisted together.

'Cool, what's that?' said Liam. He took hold of the line and tugged sharply. The branch above them bent, but the web didn't break. Liam wrapped the web around his hands, then jumped and raised his knees to his chest. 'Check it out, I'm Spider-Man!'

'I'm not sure you should be doing that,' said Jake. It wasn't the web he was worried about, so much as the tree it was attached to. The afternoon was getting on, and the October shadows were making the tree look strangely sinister and threatening.

And not just that tree, either. The whole forest seemed to be squeezing in around them, long spindly branches reaching towards them like twisting claws and withered arms.

Liam stopped swinging and released his grip. Or he tried to. The web was stuck to his hands. He hooked an arm over it to try to give himself leverage, but the webbing stuck to his arm, too.

'Well, this is annoying,' he muttered, turning to try to untangle himself. Instead, it had completely the opposite effect. The web line snared around him, pinning the top part of his arms to his side. His hands were tied together in front of him.

'Want some help?' Jake asked.

'With what?'

Jake gestured to the tangle of webbing around him. 'Well, that.'

'Hmm? Oh, no. I've got this,' Liam said. He

managed to bring his hands up and his head down enough to bite into the thread. His teeth immediately stuck to it, and he realized he was completely trapped.

'Well, 'is is awkward,' he managed to slur through his web-jammed mouth. 'Maybe 'ome 'elp 'ould 'e 'ood.'

'OK, wait there,' said Jake. Liam shot him a sarcastic look. It wasn't as if he could go anywhere. 'I need to find something to cut through the web.'

'What's happening?' Sarah called from the other side of the wall of spider silk. 'Have you found anything?'

'Er, no,' Jake lied. He knew if he told Sarah there was a giant spider's web, and Liam was trapped in it, she'd completely freak out. His eyes fell on something shiny and metallic propped up against the trunk of a tree. It was the gardener's shears. They'd be perfect for cutting through the web.

After quickly looking around to make sure their owner wasn't nearby, Jake grabbed the shears and very carefully snipped Liam free. Even with the sharp blades of the shears, it took all his strength to slice through the silk.

'I'm free!' Liam cheered, as Jake cut through a piece of the web. Liam's arm flopped loose, then immediately got tangled in another strand. 'Oh, no, spoke too soon.'

Jake lined up the shears again. He was just

preparing to snip when a rustling from deeper in the woods caught his attention. He froze, peering back into the shadows.

'What is it?' Liam asked.

'Shh,' Jake whispered. 'I think I heard something.'

Liam swallowed. 'Was it something nice?'

The sound came again—a frantic rustle of something scrabbling through the undergrowth. Or maybe the undergrowth itself coming alive!

Jake looked at the tangle of web around Liam. He looked back towards where the rustling sound was starting to draw closer.

'OK, Plan B!' he announced, stretching up and slicing the thread above Liam's head. Liam was still tied up, but at least he could run. 'Let's get out of here!' Jake yelped.

Sarah stumbled backwards as the boys launched themselves through the web wall. It made a loud *ripping* sound as they tumbled through, but then they were back on their feet and, for the second time that day, running through the cemetery towards the gate.

'Come on, Max!' Jake hollered.

Max trotted out from behind the bush, his tail wagging. He loved chasing games, and Jake looked as if he was really putting effort into this one.

The little dog was about to give chase when he

stopped and sniffed the air. His tail stopped wagging. He turned and glared into the forest, then growled way down at the back of his throat. The undergrowth rustled again, and Max decided his single growl was quite brave enough for one day, thank you very much. With a soft whine, he set off after Jake as fast as his legs would carry him.

CHAPTER EIGHT

SHADY O'GRADY'S

'What is it? What did you see?' Sarah asked as they all clattered along the path at high speed.

'Nothing,' Jake admitted. 'We didn't see anything!'

'Oh.'

They raced on.

'Then why are we running?' Sarah wondered.

'We heard a rustling sound!' Jake explained.

'Oh.'

They raced on some more.

'So?' Sarah asked. 'That could have been anything.'

Jake considered this. Back in the forest, he'd been convinced something terrifying was racing through the grass towards him, but now that he'd put some distance between himself and the trees, he was starting to wonder if maybe he'd over-reacted.

He slowed down. The others matched his pace.

'Well, I mean, I suppose it *could* have been nothing,' he conceded. 'I mean nothing dangerous.'

'Yeah,' agreed Liam. 'It was probably—yikes!'

He jumped as a small, fast-moving shape shot through his legs. The three friends watched Max disappear out of the cemetery, then heard him barking outside the holiday house's gate for someone to let him in. Clearly Max thought there was something scary lurking back there in the woods. But what exactly had they seen? Lots of spiders' webs. More than lots, in fact. 'Lots' didn't really do it justice. The last time Jake had seen so many spiders' webs in one place had been in a horror movie, and it hadn't ended well for the people involved.

So, the webs were a worry, although the man at the sweet shop—sorry, the shop that sells sweets—had mentioned a spider epidemic. In which case, maybe that was an average amount of webbing, and nothing sinister at all.

Then there was the web-shaped bush. That was ... weird. Jake couldn't really explain that one, either, but apart from the shape it had seemed just like an everyday, average bush. It hadn't tried to kill him, at least, which, considering other recent plant-based

76

events, he was taking as a good sign.

In fact, nothing had tried to kill him. Since the Creeper had the ability to control plant life, the trees would have had the perfect opportunity to make a grab for him when he was trying to free Liam. The fact that they hadn't moved to attack made him wonder if he was wrong about the gardener. Maybe he wasn't the Creeper, after all.

Jake realized he was no longer carrying the garden shears. He must have tossed them aside when he'd started running, which meant that Liam would have to stay partially wrapped up until they got back to the cottage.

'It wasn't floating,' Liam said. The expression on his face and the tone of his voice revealed how much it pained him to admit it. 'It was hanging from this stuff. That's why it was off the ground. It wasn't a ghost.'

'Oh,' said Sarah, for the third time in as many minutes. She studied the white strands wrapped around Liam's arms and upper body. 'And what is "this stuff", exactly?'

'Spider's web, we reckon,' said Liam. Sarah quickly sidestepped away.

'Really?' she said, her face turning white. She tried to smile, but it was thin and shaky, and not in the least bit convincing. 'Wow! Haha. Well, isn't that interesting?'

'Do you want me to stick some to you so you can use your big science brain to examine it?' Liam asked. He lunged for his sister, who dodged just in time to avoid a wisp of the stuff attaching itself to her face.

'No, I'm fine, thank you,' Sarah said. Her face darkened. 'By which I mean, touch me with that stuff, and I *swear* I'll kill you!'

It took Jake a long time to untangle Liam from the webbing. Sarah kept her distance by the bathroom door, ready to make a quick escape if the boys tried any funny business. She gave directions and offered support, but it was up to Jake to do all the hard work.

'No, bend his arm around,' Sarah said. 'No, the other way. Down a bit. Now loop that strand over his shoulder. The other shoulder. No, that's the same shoulder.'

Forty minutes of that, accompanied by constant complaining from Liam, and Jake finally peeled off the last silk strand. He'd worn a pair of rubber gloves to help him untangle his friend, and had carefully wound each newly-removed piece around the palm of the left glove. It now looked as if his hand had sustained some sort of terrible accident, and then been bandaged by a nurse who A) had her eyes shut, and B) wasn't actually a nurse, at all.

After removing the gloves and turning them inside out to stop the webbing sticking to anything else, Jake and the others headed downstairs. He had just finished depositing the gloves in the bin when Mum and Dad strolled in.

'Right, get yourselves organised, we're all off out,' said Dad. 'There's a pub just down the road. *Shady O'Grady's*. I thought we could all go for an early dinner.'

'At a place called *Shady O'Grady's*?' Jake asked. 'Why do I get the feeling they're not known for their fine cuisine?'

Dad smiled, smugly. 'Well, that's where you're wrong. It's the second highest-rated restaurant in Lower Larkspur-on-Sea, according to the internet.'

'Oh, right,' said Jake. He was about to take it back when a thought struck him. 'How many restaurants are in Lower Larkspur-on-Sea?' he asked, but his dad pretended he hadn't heard him.

'So, we all set, then?'

'It's two, isn't it?' asked Jake.

'Clock's ticking,' said Dad, tapping his watch and ushering them towards the stairs. 'Off you go and get ready. Dinner awaits.'

'We *are* ready,' said Jake.

Mum looked down at their muddy shoes
and jeans. Liam's back was caked in dirt, and
he had bits of shrubbery tangled in his hair.

'No,' said Mum. 'You definitely aren't. Go and
get changed. Liam, you should probably jump in the
shower.'

'You should never jump in the shower, Mrs L,' said
Liam. 'That's a recipe for disaster, that is. You should
always step in carefully.'

Jake's mum smiled in a way that suggested she
didn't know if Liam was joking or not. 'Er, right. Yes.
Well, you should step carefully into the shower, then.'

'And hurry up, all of you,' Dad said, tapping his
watch again. 'I'm starving.'

Jake stood by the bedroom window, looking at his
reflection as he tried to decide whether to do up the
top button of his shirt or not. There were no mirrors
in the bedroom. According to Dad, Lord Mason had
smashed them all, because he didn't want his wife
seeing how beautiful she was. Still, you'd have thought

that in the hundred or more years since then, someone would have nipped to IKEA to get some new ones. Jake still reckoned Dad was making the whole thing up, but if he wasn't, then Lord Mason must surely be in the running for some sort of 'Worst Husband Ever' award.

He was about to turn away from the window when he saw . . . something. A movement outside. From up here, he could only see a tiny bit of the cemetery, but quite a lot of the forest bordering it.

The evening had drawn in, and the outside world was pretty dark, especially with the bedroom light on. Jake cupped his hands around his eyes and stepped closer to the glass. He could see a couple of the closest headstones, a lot of trees and . . . wait. From up here, he could just make out the area where the weird bush was. It was dark outside, but the light from the house and the glow of the moon were just enough to see by, and up by the bush was where the movement had come from. A dark shape moved around there. Jake pressed his hands right up to the glass to try to get a better view.

Suddenly, the shape whipped around. Two glowing green eyes glared back at Jake, and he stumbled back from the window in fright. He was right, it *was* the Creeper!

From the way those horrible eyes had turned and held his gaze, Jake could tell it wasn't an accident. The Creeper knew he was there, and had been looking straight at him. Oh, this was bad. This was *very* bad.

With a *swish*, Jake pulled the curtains closed. The clanking sound of the shower had stopped, and he hopped around impatiently, waiting for Liam to return. He thought about running through to tell Sarah, but she might still be getting changed, and he'd rather face the Creeper than face *that*.

Several long, agonizing minutes later, Liam returned. He'd got himself dressed in the bathroom, and now wore a yellow T-shirt with the words, 'Please don't kill me,' printed on the front in block capitals. Despite Jake's urgent need to tell him about the Creeper, he couldn't help but stare at the T-shirt for a moment.

'What's that?' he asked.

Liam grinned. 'What, this old thing? Just a little something I had made in that printing place back home before we left. I figured I could wear it if the

Creeper ever came back. I thought he might take pity on me. But, since we're heading to a pub called *Shady O'Grady's*, I reckoned it was worth wearing it now.'

'Right,' said Jake. 'Speaking of the Creeper . . . ?'

Jake's dad appeared in the doorway behind Liam. 'Ready, boys?' he asked.

'One second, Mr L. Jake was just telling me something about . . . ' He caught Jake's expression, and quickly glanced around the room. 'About, uh, woodworm.'

Jake and his dad both frowned at the same time. 'Woodworm?' said Mr Latchford. 'Interesting. And what was it you were telling him, Jake?'

Jake's mind raced. His mouth flapped open and closed a few times. 'Uh, that they're worms . . . '

'Right,' agreed Dad.

'Who like wood?' Jake guessed.

Dad blinked. 'I see. Well, fascinating insight,' he said. 'Thanks for that. Now down you come. Sarah's already down there, and we're all ready to go.'

Jake forced a smile. Dad was standing right there, waiting for them to move. Telling Liam about the Creeper would have to wait.

As Jake and the others stepped in through the front door of *Shady O'Grady's*, the music scratched to a halt. The barman looked up from the glass he was polishing, as all eight or nine of the pub's customers turned towards the door.

'Stupid thing. It's always doing that,' said the barman. He hit the CD player with the heel of his hand and the music stuttered back into life again. Two of the customers cheerfully raised their glasses to Jake's mum and dad, then went back to their conversations.

Despite that awkward first moment, *Shady O'Grady's* was ... better than Jake had been expecting. Mind you, that wasn't saying much. His expectations had been *very* low.

He was pleasantly surprised, though. The décor was designed to look old-fashioned, but it was clean and fresh-looking, and the pub actually felt surprisingly modern. There was an extensive menu written in colourful chalks on a large blackboard behind the bar. Jake immediately spotted at least three things he liked the sound of, and even though the Creeper was still on his mind, he felt his stomach rumble in anticipation.

'In an ideal world, I'd have one of everything,' said Liam, eyeing up the menu. 'Except the salad, obviously.'

'Obviously,' agreed Jake. 'I mean, that would be mad.'

'Exactly,' said Liam.

Sarah shook her head. 'Boys!' She sighed. 'There's nothing wrong with salad.'

'Yeah, if you're a rabbit,' said Liam, then he stopped talking and sniffed the air. 'Wait, I know that smell.'

It took him a few seconds of looking to spot the little purple bag behind the bar. Once he'd spotted one, he quickly saw half a dozen others. 'They're using lavender here, too,' Liam said.

'I guess they're having a bug problem, too,' said Jake.

Sarah shuddered and glanced around her in panic. To her relief, there were no spiders to be seen. Still, she wasn't taking any chances. As soon as they'd all placed their food orders, Sarah asked the barman if she could 'borrow' one of the lavender bags.

'She doesn't like spiders,' Jake explained.

'Oh, I see,' said the barman. 'Then you'd best 'ave one, pet. Lots of spiders around this year. Most I've seen since . . . well, since ever.'

He passed a bag to Sarah. She immediately rubbed it all over her hands and face, then shoved it in her pocket.

'Thanks,' she said. She stepped away from the bar, heading to join Jake's mum and dad at a nearby table, but Jake grabbed her arm.

'I was right. He's here,' Jake whispered. 'The Creeper is here.'

Liam whipped around in panic. Sarah rolled her eyes. 'Again, not *literally* here in this room,' Sarah told him. She lowered her voice and bent in closer to Jake. 'How do you know?'

'I saw him from the bedroom window. Glowing green eyes, and all.'

'You're sure?' said Sarah.

Jake nodded. 'And that's not the worst part,' he said, shuddering at the memory of that hate-filled stare. 'He saw me, too.'

'Come on, kids!' called Jake's dad. 'We've got something to tell you.'

'Not a word about this,' Jake whispered. 'We'll talk later.'

The three friends forced awkward-looking smiles as they strolled over to the table, trying to act as naturally as possible. It wasn't particularly effective.

'What's wrong with your faces?' Dad asked. 'Are you ill?'

'Um, actually, I don't feel too well,' said Jake. 'I think maybe we should go home. As in *home* home, not the cottage. Back to Larkspur.'

'What? Already,' said Dad. 'But we only arrived yesterday. We're here until the end of the week.'

Mum didn't look particularly excited by the prospect, but she was doing her best to show a united front. 'That's right. We've still got five days left, and there's lots to do. Apparently. I mean, I haven't seen anything, but . . . ' She caught Dad's weak smile. 'But it'll be fun. I'm sure you'll be feeling right as rain in no time, Jake.'

'Besides, this will cheer you up,' Dad said. 'Your mum and me thought we might hang on here for a couple of hours after dinner. Get to know a few of the locals, sort of thing, maybe find out the best places to go, things to see, whatever.'

Mum smiled. 'So, provided you three agree to be on your best behaviour, that means you'll have the whole house to yourself for a while, so you can do what you like.'

'Within reason,' Dad quickly added. 'No trashing the place, or I'll have to pay for the damages. But, you know, you could watch telly or something.'

'Is there a telly?' asked Liam, suddenly interested. 'I didn't see a telly.'

'What? Well, I mean, I assume so,' said Dad. He looked across at Jake's mum. She shook her head. 'Oh. Right. Well, not watching telly, then, but I'm sure you could . . . ' He puffed out his cheeks and wracked his brain for inspiration. '. . . do *something*,' was the best he

87

could come up with. He smiled broadly. 'Right?'

Jake forced a smile. Normally, having the house to themselves might be fun, but not *that* house, and not with the Creeper lurking around somewhere outside.

But that was only part of the problem. If Mum and Dad were staying here, that meant that he, Liam, and Sarah would have to walk back to the cottage through the dark.

Alone.

CHAPTER NINE

THE ONSLAUGHT

Jake and Sarah were both too worried about the Creeper to eat much of their dinner. Luckily, Liam was on hand to polish off their leftovers. Dad and Mum both made jokes about Liam's stomach being a bottomless pit (he'd also packed away three desserts) and then it was time for the children to leave.

'We won't be long,' Jake's mum said.

'And no destroying anything,' Dad reminded them.

And now, a few minutes later, the three friends huddled together as they marched through the darkened streets of Lower Larkspur-on-Sea, on their way back to their holiday cottage from hell.

Lower Larkspur wasn't exactly a fantastic-looking place during the day. It had a certain faded grandeur to it that suggested it had once been a thriving seaside resort, but now most of the buildings looked old and tired.

At night, it was even worse. Half of the street lights were either flickering erratically, or off completely, casting long stretches of pavement into deep, dark pools of shadow.

The houses looked cold and unfriendly, their gardens more overgrown than Jake had noticed during the walk to the pub. Lights were on in a few windows. The flickering glow of televisions shone from several more. Liam stared longingly at these, trying to figure out what was on from just the way the light danced across the curtains. One was a gameshow, he reckoned. Another, some kind of medical drama.

'Man, I miss TV,' he mumbled.

They pressed on into the gloom, Liam watching the windows, Jake and Sarah peering into the shadowy alleyways and side streets around them. The Creeper could be lurking down any of them, just waiting to pounce.

A house ahead of them had a tall hedge around its garden. Jake made them give it a wide berth, convinced the hedge's brittle branches would make a grab for him as they passed. To his relief, its only movement was from the breeze fluttering through its leaves.

'And you're *sure* it was him?' Sarah asked. It was the fifth time she'd asked the question since they'd left *Shady O'Grady's*, and Jake answered with the same grim certainty he'd answered every other time.

'It was him,' he confirmed. 'I only saw his eyes, but that was enough. The Creeper is here, and he knows we're here, too.'

'I mean, it's a bit of a coincidence,' said Liam, tearing his eyes away from one of the flickering windows. 'You know, the Creeper being here at the same time as us?' said Liam. 'I mean, what are the chances? Unless he entered the same competition, I suppose.'

Sarah stopped walking. 'Wait! The competition!'

'What about it?' asked Jake.

'Your dad, he said he couldn't remember entering it.'

'Right.'

Sarah looked from Jake to her brother and back again. They both looked confused. She sighed. 'Well, I mean, isn't it obvious?'

'Yes!' cried Liam. 'But, erm, explain it anyway, for Jake's benefit.'

'There was no competition. Your dad can't remember entering it because he didn't,' said Sarah.

Liam nodded. 'Yep. Yep. That's exactly what I was thinking,' he said. 'Although, Jake's probably wondering, if there was no competition, how did Mr

91

L win the prize?'

'He didn't,' said Jake, as the truth finally hit him.

'Of course!' said Liam, clicking his fingers. 'Your *mum* must have entered it.'

Jake shook his head. 'No one did. Like Sarah said, there wasn't any competition. The Creeper set this whole thing up. He sent my dad the prize.'

Liam couldn't quite get his head around this. 'Did he? That was alright of him, wasn't it? Maybe he's turned over a new leaf. Pun intended.'

'He brought us here to take revenge on us,' Sarah said.

'What?' Liam spluttered. 'Why would he want to get revenge on us? What have we ever done to him?'

Jake and Sarah both stared blankly at him for a few seconds, waiting for his brain to catch up.

'Oh yeah, all that stopping his evil plans and destroying his potato army stuff,' Liam said. 'Gotcha. I take back the "new leaf" stuff. He still seems pretty mean.'

They set off again, keeping quiet as they got closer to the holiday cottage. As soon as Sarah had suggested it, Jake knew she was right about the competition. This whole thing was a set-up. The Creeper had deliberately brought them to Lower Larkspur-on-Sea—but why?

He wanted to get his own back, obviously, but why

here? Why now? Why didn't he just attack them back home? There had to be something more to it.

As they turned onto the final street, Jake's blood turned to ice in his veins. Every one of the street lights here was . . . no, not off. At first, it looked as if they were off, but there was a very dim glow coming from them, which was only noticeable if you stared really hard. It was as if someone had painted over the lamps' glass, or covered it with something.

For all the good they were doing, though, the lamps may as well have been off. The street was in near-total darkness, with only the faint glow of the moon to pick out the pavement ahead.

The three friends drew closer together as they carefully picked their way along the street. Even Liam had stopped talking, and the only sound Jake could hear was the fast-paced *thudding* of his heartbeat, and the shaky rattle of his breath.

An owl hooted suddenly from the top of a nearby tree. Liam kicked out wildly, then flailed his hands in a series of frantic karate chops.

'Relax,' Sarah hissed. She didn't sound very relaxed, herself. 'It's just an owl.'

Liam nodded. 'Yeah, but the Creeper can control those, can't he?'

'No! He controls plants,' Jake whispered.

93

'Oh, yeah,' said Liam, dropping his hands to his sides. 'Who am I thinking of, then?'

Nobody knew the answer to that, so they kept quiet as they crept the final stretch to the holiday cottage's front gate. In the dim glow of the moonlight, the place looked creepier than ever. All it needed was a rumble of thunder and a flash of lightning and it would qualify as the spookiest building Jake had ever seen.

The gate *creaked* ominously as Jake pushed it open. The children froze, listening for any sign of the Creeper. The monster didn't appear.

They tiptoed on towards the front door, Jake rummaging in his pockets for the keys his mum had given him. He was halfway along the path when he felt something brush lightly across his ankle. It was a light tickle, there one moment, gone the next. From the way Sarah and Liam had both stopped, Jake guessed they'd felt something, too.

'Did anyone just—?' Liam whispered.

'I did,' Jake replied.

'And me,' Sarah whispered.

Slowly, all three children lowered their heads and looked down at the darkened path. Sarah reached a shaking hand into her pocket and pulled out her phone. There was a soft *bleep* as she activated the torch. And there, on the path, was her worst nightmare.

The ground heaved with thousands of spiders. They scrambled and scampered over each other, writhing and scurrying across the path in all directions.

The street lights returned, flooding the garden with light. Sarah couldn't tear her eyes from the mass of arachnids all around her, but Jake and Liam both looked up at the lamps. The darkness that had been covering them wasn't paint. It was spiders! Thousands of spiders had been blocking out the lights!

All along the street, the army of creepy-crawlies released their grips and dropped away from the glass. They fell lightly to the ground, and Jake imagined them closing in from all directions, racing towards the garden.

'Move!' he yelped, turning and racing towards the door. He was fumbling with the keys when disaster struck! He tripped, stumbled, and the keys slipped from his fingers. They landed right in the middle of the path, and were immediately buried by the heaving carpet of arachnids.

'No!' Sarah cried.

'I'll get them!' said Liam. He thrust his hand into the squirming mass and eight or more of the arachnids immediately began clambering up his arm.

Sarah and Jake hopped up onto the front step.

There were fewer of the bugs here, and they frantically slapped at their legs, trying to knock away the dozens of spiders climbing up them.

'Get them off! Get them off!' Sarah squealed, thrashing and kicking. Jake cleared the spiders off his own legs, then turned his attention to helping Sarah.

Liam charged at them, thrusting the keys at Jake. His arms and neck were covered in creepy-crawlies. As soon as Jake grabbed the keys, Liam spun on the spot, scratching and clawing at himself to get the bugs off.

'Not so fast, you eight-legged freaks!' Liam yelped, flicking four or five particularly large specimens off the front of his T-shirt. He caught another one before it could climb into his ear, although what it was planning to get up to in there, he had no idea. Nothing good, probably.

Jake got the door open and the three friends tumbled inside. As soon as Sarah and Liam were safely in, Jake slammed the door behind them, and locked it, for good measure. He was pretty sure spiders couldn't operate door handles, but it wasn't a chance he was willing to take.

They stood in silence for a moment, panting heavily as they tried to get their breath back. The only light was coming in through the windows, and the darkness

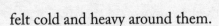

felt cold and heavy around them.

It was Jake who was the first to speak.

'OK, so what was *that* about?' he wheezed. 'That's not a spider epidemic. It's a full-scale spider plague!'

'Hroof!' Liam yelped. He straightened suddenly, his eyes wide in surprise.

Jake blinked. 'Sorry, what?'

'Aroowra! Breumf!' Liam began to hop around, beating at his chest like some kind of demented gorilla. Sarah and Jake both watched him, the horrors of the garden briefly forgotten.

'What are you doing?' Sarah demanded. 'This is not the time for mucking around.'

'Raaaueergh! Meeeep!'

Liam tore at his T-shirt and heaved it over his head. Sarah screamed when she spotted the spiders crawling all over her brother's chest and back. Jake snatched the T-shirt from his friend's hands, then used it to whip the spiders away. The bugs fell to the floor, then immediately split into three groups. Each group picked one of the children and mounted a charge.

They all reacted instinctively and began stomping on the bugs as they got closer. Several seconds of frenzied foot-thumping later, and the spiders were no longer a problem. At least, the few that had made it inside weren't, but there were still plenty more outside to deal with.

'This has to be something to do with the Creeper,' Jake panted. 'There's no way this is natural.'

'Jake, look!' Sarah whispered. Her hand was raised, the finger shaking as she pointed towards the letter box. It had opened, just a little, but enough for five or six more spiders to start crawling through.

'Sorry, no cold-callers!' said Liam, kicking the door and squishing the bugs against the wood. Jake grabbed one of the house's many ugly ornaments and wedged it into the letter box gap, blocking it up.

'That should hold them,' Jake said, but when Sarah flicked on the lights, he realized he was completely, utterly, hopelessly wrong.

'Um, want to bet?' Liam whispered. He wasn't scared of spiders, but there was a wobble in his voice that told Jake he was terrified right now. And Jake couldn't blame him.

Spiders were forcing their way in through cracks in the ancient walls. They squeezed through gaps in the skirting boards, forced their way through the narrow spaces around the window frames, and dropped down from the ornate, old light-fittings.

'Find something to block them with!' Jake cried, spinning on the spot to try to find something— anything—that could prevent the spiders getting inside.

Liam grabbed his T-shirt back, cracked it like a whip at an approaching spider horde, then pulled it back on.

'Here, use this!' said Sarah, as she came running back from the kitchen. She'd moved so quickly, Jake hadn't even seen her go. He caught the roll of cling film she tossed his way and shrugged. It wasn't exactly an indestructible force field, but it was better than nothing.

'Liam, grab an end,' Jake barked, unrolling a long strip of the stuff. 'Liam?'

He looked around, but Liam was nowhere to be seen. Sarah drew in a deep breath and forced down her rising panic. 'Here, I'll do it,' she said, catching the offered end of the transparent wrap. She and Jake layered a strip across one of the biggest cracks in the walls, then used another three pieces to cover the window.

At first, it seemed to be holding, but then the weight of the spiders building up behind it became too much and the cling film peeled away, letting the bugs inside.

'It's no use,' Sarah sobbed. 'We can't stop them!'

Liam's roar came out of nowhere, startling Sarah and Jake. 'GRENADE!'

Something flew through the air right beside Jake's head. He reacted instantly, grabbing Sarah and pulling her behind an armchair. They both covered their ears and screwed their eyes shut.

Nothing happened.

They opened their eyes to find Liam standing over them, looking down. 'Well, I mean, it wasn't *actually* a real grenade,' Liam said. 'Where would I have got one of them?' He thought for a moment. 'That little shop, probably. I mean, it sells everything else, doesn't it?'

'What are you talking about?' Sarah hissed. 'Why did you scream, "grenade" at us?!'

Liam wrinkled his nose. 'I wouldn't say I "screamed" exactly. I'd say I sort of bellowed dramatically.'

'*Liam!*'

'Right, yeah, sorry,' said Liam. He gestured for them to stand up. 'See for yourself.'

Cautiously, Jake and Sarah emerged from behind the chair. A single purple bag sat in the middle of the floor, all alone. The spiders were giving it a wide berth. Several dozen of them seemed to be running away from the stuff.

'Natural insect repellent, that's what you said,' Liam said, grinning at his sister. 'And you say I never listen to you.'

'I never say that,' said Sarah.

Liam shrugged. 'Oh, don't you? I wouldn't really know, I'm never listening.'

Jake headed for the stairs. 'We need more of that stuff. It's our only chance.'

They tore through all the bedrooms, pulling open every drawer and wardrobe and gathering the lavender bags from every one. By the time they had finished the search, they were equipped with half a dozen of the bags each.

'OK, so now we've got a weapon,' said Jake. 'At least we can fight back.'

'First things first,' said Sarah. Bending down, she tucked the bottom of her jeans into her socks. 'That should help keep them out.'

'Good idea,' said Jake. He and Liam both did the same. They had just straightened up when a terrible thought hit Jake with such force it almost knocked him onto Sarah's bed.

'Oh, no,' he whispered. 'Oh no, no, no.'

'What?' asked Sarah. 'What's the matter? What's wrong?'

Jake looked up. His face was white and his hands were shaking. He could barely even bring himself to say the words.

'Max!' he whispered. 'He's still downstairs. He must be in the kitchen.'

Sarah shook her head. 'He wasn't. I was in there. I didn't see him.'

'It's fine,' said Liam. 'Jake's dad put him into the back garden before we all went out to the . . .'

Liam's voice tailed off into silence as he realized what he was saying. 'Oooh, boy.'

Jake threw himself out onto the upstairs landing. He took the stairs three at a time, then jumped the last few, waving the lavender bags in front of him. The hall carpet was buried beneath a mass of spider bodies. The walls and ceiling heaved with them, too, and it looked as if the whole hallway was coming to life.

Jake raced into the kitchen and pulled open the back door. He heard Max's high-pitched whimpers immediately, but the garden was too dark to see where the little dog was.

There was a switch mounted beside the door frame. Jake flicked it and a security light outside blinked into life. Liam and Sarah arrived just in time to see the full horror of the scene illuminated in a blinding white glow.

Max was lying on the back path. At least, they assumed it was Max. Thousands of spiders were cocooning a wriggling, struggling, Max-sized shape, which was emitting some decidedly Max-like yelps and yips.

'Get away from him, you monsters!' Jake roared, leaping onto the path and charging towards his helpless dog. Liam hurried out after him, and the sight of Max in distress made even Sarah forget her fear for the moment. She bounded out after the boys, tossing three of her lavender bags ahead of her and driving some of the spiders away.

Liam threw a couple of his bags so they landed either side of Max. The spiders that had been wrapping him up scrambled away, leaving the way clear for Jake to help the little dog out. Max's teeth tore at the webbing as he desperately tried to free himself.

The dog's eyes were covered, but his little nose twitched as he picked up Jake's scent. Even through the cocoon, Jake saw Max's tail begin to wag. He pulled and heaved at the webbing, and Max let out an excited *woof* of joy as his head emerged from the webbing.

They'd done it! Max was safe! Jake felt his heart soar. This was definitely a victory. Maybe, just maybe, he thought, things were going to be OK, after all.

But he was wrong.

CHAPTER TEN

HAIL TO THE KING

'Uh, OK, so that's not good,' said Liam.

Jake, Sarah, and the now untangled Max turned and saw what Liam was looking at. The whole back wall of the house was now one big mass of spiders. They swarmed down over the sloping roof, scrambled over the drainpipes, and amassed on the walls.

The back door was still standing open, but the kitchen looked to be in total darkness. It was only when Jake looked more closely that he realized why. The floor and walls were covered several centimetres deep in creepy-crawlies. There was no way to get back inside the house.

'We need to get help,' Sarah whimpered, her earlier courage fading rapidly. 'Your mum and dad. The police.'

'Rentokil,' Liam suggested. 'Or, like, anyone with a flamethrower.'

With the house now out of bounds, there was only one way to go. The garden backed straight on to the cemetery. If they could get through there, they could make it to the street and run for help.

Jake scooped Max up and quickly explained his plan. He had to admit that 'plan' was a generous word for what he had in mind. The entire scheme basically involved opening the gate and running as fast as they could. It was hardly a masterclass in military strategy, but it was the best he could come up with at short notice.

Liam and Sarah both agreed at once. Anything that involved getting as far from the spiders as possible was a good plan, as far as Sarah was concerned, and even Liam, who had never been scared of spiders before, now never wanted to see another one for as long as he lived.

'OK, so we stick close together, get to the street, and just leg it as fast as we can back to the pub,' Jake said. 'My mum and dad will know what to do.'

'Will they?' said Sarah.

Jake shook his head. 'Probably not. But at least we won't have to deal with all this on our own.'

'And the pub will have a flamethrower,' said Liam.

Jake and Sarah both hesitated. 'Why would they have a flamethrower?' Jake asked.

'Well, it's the law, isn't it?' said Liam. 'Bars and restaurants and all that, they've got to have a flamethrower.'

Sarah and Jake exchanged a confused look, and then Sarah raised her eyebrows. 'Hang on, are you thinking of a fire extinguisher?'

Liam considered this. 'Hmm. Maybe. Is that different?'

'It's literally the opposite thing,' said Jake. He glanced at the approaching spider horde, then hurried for the gate. 'Now come on, before these things catch up with us. They might have little legs, but they can move pretty fast.'

The children ran out into the cemetery. The woods towered above them over on the right, tall and sinister in the darkness. Max growled in Jake's arms, his eyes scanning the ground around them for more spiders. Now that he was well out of the bugs' reach, he felt it was safe enough to do a bit of growling. Maybe he'd bark a couple of times, he hadn't decided yet.

The grass twisted and tangled around their ankles as they ran, reminding Jake that the spiders weren't the only scary thing lurking around here. The Creeper was nearby somewhere. He had no idea what he'd do if they ran into him now, but it almost certainly involved losing bladder control.

It was a relief when they made it off the grass and onto the path. They clattered down it for the third time that day, then skidded to a stop when they neared the graveyard gate. The path beyond it moved liked a fast-flowing river towards them. There had to be ten thousand spiders out there. A hundred thousand, maybe. The way out was blocked! Their only escape route was cut off.

'No!' Jake groaned. 'Now what?'

'This way!' Sarah urged, running up the path in the opposite direction. 'I think there's another gate at the other end. If we can reach it before the spiders do, we can get out that way.'

Jake wasn't sure he liked that plan. The path would lead them very close to where he'd seen the Creeper. This had 'trap' written all over it. But what choice did they have? It was either run, or drown in a squirming sea of eight-legged critters.

He launched himself after Sarah and Liam, Max growling and barking over his shoulder at the pursuing horde. They sprinted on, putting a decent amount of distance between themselves and the spiders.

They were halfway up the path when they spotted a large shadowy shape. It emerged from behind a gravestone, its hairy coat glinting in the moonlight as it bounded towards them on its eight legs.

Wait.

What?!

Sarah stopped running, immediately going completely rigid with fear. The thing scuttling towards them was roughly the height of a big dog, but as the light shone off its oily exoskeleton and eight unblinking eyes, the terrible truth became clear.

It was a spider.

No, that didn't do it justice. It was the biggest, most terrifying spider the world had ever seen.

And it was headed straight for them!

More specifically, it was headed straight for Sarah. She stood stock still, her eyes wide and staring, her feet rooted to the spot as the giant arachnid charged at her.

'Sis, look out!' Liam warned, but Sarah either didn't hear him, or was too terrified to do anything about it.

The eight-legged monster was almost on her. There was no time to lose.

Liam threw himself at his sister, waving a lavender bag at the spider as he knocked Sarah out of its path. 'Watch it, Leggy,' he warned the bug. 'I've got the smell of old ladies here, and I'm not afraid to use it.'

The spider's powerful mandibles lunged for Liam's hand. They snapped shut around the lavender bag and wrenched it from Liam's grip. The mandibles ground together, tearing the bag apart and spilling its contents onto the path. The spider didn't seem to be affected by the stuff at all, probably due to its sheer size.

'OK, so that's not good,' Liam groaned, then he cried out in shock as the monstrous arachnid jumped on him, knocking him over and pinning him to the ground. Those coarse, wiry mandibles edged closer to Liam's face. He tried to pull away, but he was squashed between the spider and the path, and there was nowhere for him to go.

'Hey, leave him alone!' yelled Jake. He ran for the spider and kicked it hard on the side. It felt worryingly solid, and the kick didn't seem to bother it much.

He kicked again, even harder this time. The spider hissed and spun around, its eight eyes glaring hatred at Jake, who suddenly realized that attacking the brute might not have been the most sensible idea he'd ever had.

Its legs twitched and the giant arachnid launched itself towards him, mandibles snapping as it hurtled through the air. Jake dived sideways just in the nick of time and landed heavily on the grass. Max yelped as he tumbled from Jake's arms.

The grass wriggled and squirmed beneath Jake, and he imagined hundreds of spiders down there, crawling out from between the blades. But no, it wasn't spiders that were moving, it was the grass itself. It began to tangle itself around him, pinning him in place, holding him steady as the spider-monster crept towards him.

Jake heaved frantically at the grass. He tore several clumps of the stuff free, but for every strand he removed, a dozen more wrapped around him. 'H-help!' he cried, but Liam was still dazed, still trying to get to his feet, still too far away to reach him in time.

The moon emerged from behind a cloud, casting its full eerie glow across the spider's hideous face. Jake felt his whole body tighten in terror, and time seemed to grind into slow motion.

The spider's eight glassy black eyes were cold and emotionless as they locked onto Jake. There was no remorse or pity in them anywhere, and as its mandibles twitched hungrily, Jake feared his

110

time had come. This thing was going to eat him, and there was nothing he could do about it.

The spider lunged and time sped up again. Jake braced himself for the pain, then wheezed out a sigh of relief when a thick, heavy branch *thwacked* down on top of the spider's head.

'Leave my friend alone!' Sarah spat. She swung with the stick again, hitting the spider on one of its legs. It let out a short, sharp screech, then spun around.

Before it could attack, a furry shape shot past Jake in a blur of speed and angry barks. Max yipped and snarled at the spider, charging towards it, then quickly backing away. The monster seemed to lose interest in Sarah, and turned to face the little dog, instead. It hissed noisily at Max, who immediately stopped barking.

From the look on Max's face, he had clearly come to the conclusion that he'd made a terrible mistake. What had he been thinking? This thing was massive!

With a panicky yelp, Max about-turned and shot off into the darkness. The spider charged after him, barging past Liam just as he stood up, almost knocking him over again.

'Help, I'm stuck!' Jake said. Liam and Sarah both hurried to his side and helped tear him free of his grassy restraints. As soon as he was free, they hopped onto the path, keeping their distance from the rogue greenery.

Jake peered into the darkness, searching for any sign of his dog, but Max and the monstrous arachnid were both gone.

'Did anyone else just see a massive spider?' Liam gasped.

'What do you mean, "Did anyone else see a massive spider"?' Sarah snapped. 'Of course we did! It tried to attack us!'

Liam almost looked relieved. 'OK, so I didn't imagine it, then. That's good.' He thought about this for a moment. 'Actually, no, I'd prefer it if I had imagined it. That thing was *real*?!'

Jake nodded. 'Afraid so. The question is, where did it come from?'

'I think I can probably answer that,' said Sarah. She gestured up the path to the web-shaped bush. It was completely covered in the same white webbing they'd found at the forest's edge earlier. 'That bush looks like some sort of egg sac.'

'Wait!' said Liam.

Everyone waited.

'Why?' asked Sarah, after several seconds had passed.

'I'm . . . I think I had an idea,' Liam said, his eyes

darting left and right as he tried to find it again. 'Oh, yes, got it! I think the spider was the ghost I saw in the woods.'

Sarah frowned. 'I thought that was floating,' she said, then it clicked. 'No, not floating. Hanging from that web strand you found.'

'Exactly!' said Liam.

While they'd been talking, Jake had approached the bush. It was completely cocooned in webbing, but he could make out three large bulges beneath the silk. The bulges moved around in a highly disturbing way, and Jake suddenly found the image of millions of baby spiders forcing its way into his brain. He jumped back from the bush, as if he'd just been electrocuted.

'Uh, guys, I think we have a problem,' he whispered.

'Oh, you think so?' said Sarah, as she and Liam joined him beside the bush. 'The house is *literally* covered in bugs, and the King of All Spiders is currently loose somewhere, probably hunting us down right now. I think "problem" is a bit of an understatement, don't you?'

Jake half-smiled at her. 'Good point,' he said. 'And thanks, by the way.'

'For what?'

'For whacking it with your big stick,' Jake said.

Sarah looked down at the branch in her hand, as if

113

seeing it for the first time. 'Oh. Right,' she said, then a grin spread across her face. 'Yeah, I did, didn't I? That thing didn't know what hit it!'

Liam took the stick from her hands and approached the bush. The egg sacs bulged unpleasantly beneath the webbing. 'We should whack these things, too!' he said. 'Before all the spiders break out.'

'Liam, stop!' Jake cried. 'Think about what you're saying.'

Liam hesitated. 'Huh? What do you mean?'

Sarah sighed. 'In order to *stop* the spiders breaking out of the egg sacs, you're going to smash them with a big stick,' she said. 'In what world does that seem like a good idea?'

When it was clear that Liam was still confused, Jake explained. 'If you smash the sacs, the spiders get out.'

'Oh. Right. Yes,' said Liam, lowering the branch. 'Well, why didn't you just say that in the first place?'

'Do you think these are big ones?' Jake asked.

'They don't look that big,' said Liam.

'No, I mean, do you think they'll grow into big ones?'

Sarah peered at the egg sacs. 'They're definitely much larger than anything I've ever read about, so . . . I think they will.'

114

'We have to do something,' said Jake. Lower Larkspur-on-Sea was already Spider Central. Adding another few million to the mix wasn't exactly going to improve the situation.

'Pity the shop's all out of insect repellent,' said Liam.

Sarah let out a little gasp. 'Wait, that's it!' she cried. 'Liam, you're a . . . Well, no, I was going to say "genius" but that's obviously not true. Liam, you're a bit smarter than I thought you were!'

'I am?' said Liam, frowning. 'I mean, yes. Obviously. Of course I am.' He smiled, uncertainly. 'Uh, what makes you say that, exactly?'

'I know where to find insect repellent,' Sarah announced.

Jake almost cheered. 'You do? That's brilliant! Where?'

Sarah shifted uncomfortably. 'Well, you see, there's good news and there's bad news. Like I said, I know where to find some,' she said, then she swallowed nervously and her voice became a shaky whisper. 'The bad news is, it's down in the basement.'

'What?' Jake spluttered. 'But—'

'That's right,' said Sarah. A cool breeze swirled around the children, making all three of them shiver. 'If we want to get the bug spray, we're going to have to go back into the house.'

CHAPTER ELEVEN

ALL MONSTERS TOGETHER

The three friends stood in silence for a long time, considering their next move. The egg sacs had to be destroyed, and unless they stumbled upon one of those flamethrowers Liam had spoken about earlier, the insecticide spray was their best chance.

Last time they'd seen the house, though, it had been positively heaving with creepy-crawlies. Going back in there was pretty much the craziest idea they'd ever had—and that was really saying something. All things considered, Jake would rather take his chances with the giant spider than be covered by thousands of little ones. What if he tripped? They'd cocoon him in their webs. Or worse, clamber up his nose and down his throat and . . .

He shuddered, and tried to push the thought away. What choice did he have? The house was their only hope.

'Fine,' he said, reluctantly. 'I'll go.'

'OK!' replied Liam, cheerfully. Jake shot him a sideways look.

'What?'

'OK!' Liam repeated.

'Right,' said Jake. 'I mean . . . aren't you going to try to talk me out of it, or anything?'

Liam shook his head. 'No. Don't think so.'

Jake shifted uncomfortably. 'Oh. You're not going to volunteer to go in my place, then?'

'No way!' Liam snorted. 'Go back in there? That would be mad. I'd rather just let the spiders take over the world than go back in there, to be honest. I mean, it was creepy enough before it was filled with bugs, imagine what it's like in there now.'

'OK, OK!' Jake said.

'I'll go.'

Jake and Liam both turned to Sarah. She was shifting her weight nervously from foot to foot, flexing her fingers in and out as she tried to control her breathing.

'What?' said Jake, convinced he must have been hearing things.

117

'I said I'll go,' Sarah repeated. 'I'm the only one who knows where the stuff is.'

Jake shook his head. 'It's in the basement. You told us.'

'It's a big basement,' Sarah pointed out. She smiled weakly. 'Believe me, I don't want to go. I'd do anything not to go, actually. But it's our only chance.'

Jake was filled with conflicting emotions. Part of him was relieved not to be going down there into the basement, but another part didn't want his friend to have to do it. He knew how scared Sarah was of spiders. Going back into the house would be like her worst nightmare come true.

Still, what she was saying made sense. Jake had no idea where the pesticide spray was. It could take him several minutes to find it in the basement, and that was assuming the spider army hadn't invaded there, too. If they had, he might never find the stuff in time. Every second wasted was a second closer to the egg sacs hatching open.

'Are you sure?' Jake asked.

Sarah shook her head. 'Not by a long shot,' she admitted. She drew in a deep breath. 'But I'll give it a go.'

'I'll come with you,' said Jake, but Sarah shook her head.

'I've got a plan, but it won't work for both of us,' she said. 'Give me your lavender bags.'

The boys handed over their bags without question, and watched as she tore them open and poured the contents over herself. She tipped some into her hair, rubbed some into her clothing, and tucked a few dried sprigs into her socks.

Realizing what she was doing, Jake and Liam both helped. They worked quickly, and in just over a minute, there wasn't a patch of Sarah that didn't positively reek of old ladies' perfume.

'Hopefully this should keep them at bay,' she said.

'It will,' said Jake, trying to be as positive as possible. 'Get in, get the stuff, and get back out. We'll be waiting right outside.'

Sarah shook her head. 'Stay here. Watch the egg sacs, in case they hatch.'

'Right. And what do we do if they do and lots of mutant spiders come out?' Liam asked.

Sarah thought about this. 'Try not to die, I suppose.' She smiled nervously. 'If I need you, you'll hear me screaming. Trust me. Half the world will hear me screaming!'

Liam chewed his lip and stepped in closer to his sister. His face was more sombre and serious than Jake had ever seen it. 'Hey, sis, I want you to know something,' he said.

'It's fine, Liam. You don't have to say anything,' said Sarah.

'No, I do,' Liam insisted. He took a deep breath. 'I need to tell you . . . if, you know, the worst happens, I'm having your laptop.'

Sarah stared at him for a few seconds, then grinned and punched him on the arm. 'It's password protected,' she told him. 'So good luck getting into it.'

Liam smiled back, then threw his arms around her and hugged her. 'Good luck,' he whispered, then the smell of lavender became too much and he stepped away. 'By the way, you totally smell like Nan.'

'I hope not,' said Sarah. 'Nan's been dead for four years.'

Liam smirked. 'Exactly,' he said, then he jumped back to avoid another punch.

Sarah took another deep breath and nodded. 'Right. Here goes,' she said. Then, with a final salute, she about-turned and marched purposefully down the hill.

The boys watched her go until she was gobbled up by the darkness. 'She's going to be OK,' Jake said, although he wasn't sure who he was trying to convince.

'Yeah. Yeah, she's going to be fine,' Liam agreed. He cleared his throat. 'On a completely different note, I don't suppose you know the password for her laptop, do you?'

Despite everything, Jake couldn't help but smile. 'I think it's *Liam is an insensitive jerk*,' he said. 'Or something along those lines.'

'Thanks,' said Liam. 'I'll try that.'

Suddenly, from somewhere behind them, there came a low, sinister hiss. Both boys froze, too terrified to move a muscle.

'Did you hear that?' Liam whispered.

Jake swallowed. 'Yes.'

'Oh. I hoped I was imagining it this time.'

Jake risked shaking his head, just a fraction. 'No. Afraid not.'

'Right.'

They stood there in silence for several long, panic-filled seconds.

'It's the big spider, isn't it?' Liam whispered.

'Probably.'

'Should we look?'

Jake groaned. 'Probably.'

'OK, on three,' said Liam. 'One. Two . . . Two and a half.' He inhaled and held it. 'Three.'

Jake turned. Liam didn't.

'Oh, well thanks very much,' Jake hissed.

'Sorry,' said Liam. 'Is it the spider?'

Another voice replied. 'It is.' A pair of green eyes

121

illuminated in the darkness. Jake's legs almost gave out beneath him as the Creeper stepped from the gloom, the King of All Spiders scurrying along beside him. 'But it isn't alone.'

'T-tell me that isn't the Creeper,' Liam stammered.

Jake licked his lips, which were suddenly very dry. 'It's not the Creeper.'

Liam relaxed. 'Oh, thank God for that,' he said, turning. His relief was short-lived, though. 'It *is* the Creeper!' he yelped.

'Yeah, sorry, I lied,' said Jake.

The Creeper had never exactly been noted for his good looks, but in the glow of the moon he looked even worse than usual. The pale white light made his bark-like skin look even more pitted and rough than usual. His head was completely bald, aside from the occasional sprouting leaf, and as he twisted his mouth into a grin, his brown and yellow teeth were revealed in their full horror.

'Now then, boys,' the Creeper said, in a voice that was part-whisper, part-giggle. 'What *are* we going to do with you two?'

Sarah reached the cottage's back gate, and immediately regretted the decision to volunteer. The path was carpeted by spiders from one end to the other. They covered the gate, the back step, and painted at least as much of the kitchen as she could see. Probably all the bits she couldn't see, too.

She turned to run away, but then forced her feet to stop. There was no other way to stop this epidemic. Their only possible chance was down there in the basement, and she was the only one who could reach it.

Slowly, shakily, she reached for the gate. As her hand approached, the nearest spiders scarpered, leaving a clear patch of wood. Sarah let out a sob of relief, but tried not to get her hopes up just yet.

She pushed open the gate and shuffled onto the path. The heaving mass of bugs parted before her, leaving a clear route to the back door. Sarah felt her hopes soar. The lavender was working! The spiders were keeping their distance.

She continued along the path, cautiously at first, but quickly getting bolder. As soon as the bugs caught a whiff of the lavender smell, they darted out of her way.

She made a mental note to invest all her pocket money in lavender-scented perfume if and when she ever got home, then plodded up the back step and ventured into the house.

Once inside, Sarah felt that urge to run away again. The inside of the house was worse than she'd feared. The floor, walls, ceiling, worktops, and appliances were all covered with a living carpet of creepy-crawlies. It was like being in the middle of a storm cloud, with nothing but squirming darkness in every direction.

'You can do this, Sarah,' she whispered, clenching her fists and gritting her teeth. 'You can do this.'

She took a step forward. A foot-sized patch of clear lino appeared as the bugs scurried away from the lavender stench. Sarah continued on another few steps, then risked a glance back. The empty spaces on the lino had already closed over as the spiders rushed back in. So, the lavender was scaring them away, but it didn't keep them away for long. She just had to hope the smell didn't wear off her soon, or she'd be in big trouble.

Twelve slow, careful steps later, Sarah made it to the door leading down to the basement. A particularly nasty-looking big bug was perched on the handle, its long legs gripping the metal. Under any normal circumstances, the sight of a spider that large would be enough to send Sarah packing, but she'd come this far, and there was no way she was turning back now, even if every one of her instincts was screaming at her to run.

Besides, this thing was a fraction of the size of the one they'd seen outside, and she'd been brave enough to hit that with a stick. She could definitely cope with this one.

Steeling her nerve, she reached for the door handle. The spider drew back a little, but didn't retreat all the way.

'Shoo!' she urged. 'Go on, get away!'

The spider reared up onto six legs and waved the other two threateningly. Something about the bug waving its fists at her made her let out a snort of laughter. It was big, admittedly, but it was just a spider. What could it do?

'Apart from help all its friends wrap me up in webs, or bury me alive in creepy-crawlies,' she muttered, then tried not to picture them swarming over her, forcing their way up her nose and into her mouth.

With a quick, panicky flick of a finger, she sent the bug flying through the air. It dropped into the wriggling mass on the floor and Sarah lost sight of it.

'And don't come back!' she warned, then she edged open the basement door and stepped down into the cold, silent darkness.

125

'What are you doing here, Creeper?' Jake demanded, spitting out the monster's name as if it left a bad taste in his mouth.

The Creeper grinned and flexed his long, clawed fingers in and out. Beside him, the giant spider's glassy eyes flicked from Jake to Liam and back again. Jake could tell it was desperate for them to try something so it could attack. He just hoped Liam wasn't about to do anything stupid.

What was he thinking? This was Liam he was talking about. Of *course* he was going to do something stupid. Jake stepped closer to his friend and took hold of his sleeve. If Liam tried to launch a direct attack, Jake would pull him back.

'That's a very interesting question, boy,' the Creeper said. 'The truth of it is, I belong here.'

Jake shrugged. 'Yeah, well ever since we met you I've wanted to see you in a graveyard,' he said. 'I just didn't expect you to be standing up.'

'Not in the graveyard, you imbecile. Here. In this dreadful little town.'

Jake frowned. 'You belong in Lower Larkspur-on-

Sea?'

The Creeper hissed angrily. 'I *am* Lower Larkspur-on-Sea!'

Liam blinked several times and opened his mouth to ask a question. Jake stopped him. 'He doesn't literally mean he's the whole town,' Jake explained. He turned his attention back to the half-man, half-plant. 'So, what? You used to live here?'

'Born and raised,' the Creeper confirmed. 'I spent fifteen miserable years in this dump. Fifteen years of being laughed at and mocked and bullied by the brainless buffoons who inhabit it.'

'Why would anyone bully you?' Liam asked. 'You're so funny and likeable.' He glanced from Jake to the Creeper and back again. 'That was sarcasm, by the way. Do you think he noticed?'

'Silence!' the Creeper roared, and the spider shifted its weight onto its back legs as if getting ready to leap. 'My family has been here for generations—my ancestor, Lord Mason, founded this wretched place.'

'Wait, you're related to Lord Mason?' gasped Jake.

'The crazy old guy from the paintings?' said Liam. He nodded. 'Actually, that doesn't surprise me *at all*.'

'I knew he looked familiar,' said Jake.

'Of course, after the . . . unfortunate business with his wife, and the rumours that followed, he felt it

127

best to change his name, and so Lord Mason became simply Ernest Hemlock,' the Creeper explained.

Jake and Liam both slapped themselves on the forehead at the same time. 'Of course. *Hemlock*, not *Heviot*,' said Jake. 'That was what the headstone said.'

'You should really get that cleaned up,' Liam told the Creeper. 'The writing's pretty faded.'

'Shut up!' the Creeper warned. He clenched his fists, his eyes flaring bright green. 'Ugh, I'd forgotten how annoying you two are.'

'Oh, which reminds me,' said Liam. He pointed to the 'Please don't kill me' message that was printed on his T-shirt. 'If you could bear this in mind, I'd really appreciate it.'

The spider moved to lunge, but a wave from the Creeper's hand stopped it. Jake's eyes narrowed. 'How are you doing that? How can you be controlling it? I thought your power only worked on plants?'

'Yes, but the power of my plants works on other things,' the Creeper explained. He gestured to the web-covered bush behind him. 'This specimen can only be found in one remote jungle in Venezuela. It's so rare it doesn't even have a name. Do you want to know what it does?'

'Uh, probably not,' said Liam, but the Creeper ignored him.

'Firstly, it attracts spiders. Nothing unusual there, of course, lots of plants do that. But this one—thanks to a few genetic alterations by me—does something truly incredible.'

Jake guessed what the Creeper was going to say before he said it. 'It makes them grow big,' he gasped.

The Creeper looked a little annoyed that his big moment had been stolen, but nodded. 'Lucky guess.' He gestured to the monstrous arachnid at his side and began slowly approaching the boys. 'But not only does it make them bigger, as they grow, its pollen infiltrates their mutated spider brains. I can control that pollen.'

'Which means you can control the spiders,' Jake realized.

'What about the ones in the house, though?' said Liam. 'They're not massive. How is he controlling them?'

'Simple!' crowed the Creeper.

'The big spider's doing it,' Jake guessed. 'He controls the big one, and the big one controls the smaller ones.'

'Will you *please* stop spoiling my big moments?' the Creeper snapped. 'But yes. Once my prize specimen emerged, spiders came from all over to pay homage to their new king. And this is just the beginning. Once these egg sacs hatch, the spiders within will rapidly grow, and I'll have control of them, too. Imagine it.

Hundreds of these things flooding the streets, each attracting their own million-strong army of eight-legged little followers, together inflicting my glorious revenge on the witless, pathetic people of Lower Larkspur-on . . .'

SQUELCH.

The Creeper looked down. Smeared into the grass beneath his feet was a squidgy pile of dog poo. Liam had to bite his lip to stop himself laughing.

'Whoops, sorry,' said Jake. 'I think that was Max. I forgot to come back and clean it up.'

The Creeper's expression became one of pure fury. 'I brought you here to witness my glorious revenge on the people in this dump. I was going to kill everyone else first, and leave you three until last.'

'That's nice of you,' said Liam.

'Not really. I was going to force you to watch everyone else die. I was going to terrify and torture you, and then kill you all slowly.'

Liam wrinkled his nose. 'Yeah, that's less nice.'

The Creeper's green eyes narrowed menacingly. 'But I see now that was a mistake. I should have killed you first.'

Liam and Jake both took a step back as the Creeper advanced once more. 'Luckily for me, it is a mistake that will be all too easy to rectify!'

CHAPTER TWELVE

BUG BATTLE

The steps creaked as Sarah crept down into the basement. Reaching into her pocket, she took out her phone so she could use its torch, but as she switched it on she caught the briefest glimpse of a flashing battery symbol, and then the screen turned dark.

'Great,' she whispered.

The only light came from the top of the stairs and the half-open window up by the basement ceiling. The cat must have been back and it hadn't closed properly, allowing a sliver of moonlight to pick out yet more spiders swarming over every surface.

She hoped the cat was OK. If it had come in here looking for another eight-legged snack, it would have got a very nasty surprise.

Luckily, the lavender seemed to be doing its job. The spiders were keeping their distance, and hurriedly parted as Sarah stepped down onto the hard stone floor. She'd hoped to spot the pesticide can as soon as she got down here, but in the half-light, and what with everything being buried beneath a mountain of spiders, it wasn't as easy as she thought.

She tried to retrace her steps from last time. She'd reached the bottom of the stairs, and then the spider had dropped on her head. She shuddered and glanced up at the ceiling above her. Several ancient pipes criss-crossed over it, barely visible beneath the crawling horde.

'OK, think, Sarah. What happened next?' she whispered, trying to focus on the important parts of the memory and block out the bug-based bits.

After the little brute had dropped on her, she'd stumbled, tripped, and fallen into a rack of shelving somewhere over . . . aha!

She spotted the broken shelves. They were tucked into the darkest corner in the whole basement, which was unfortunate, as it meant she'd have to rummage around in the pile of scattered tins and bottles on the floor. Lavender or not, she really didn't fancy rooting around in the dark with her bare hands. There was no saying what she might touch.

But she didn't exactly have many options. Unless . . .

Sarah looked back at the window. If she could pull open the rest of the way, it might let in enough light for her to spot the bug spray. It was worth a try, at least.

Picking her way across the squirming floor, she reached for the window. Her fingers brushed against it, but she wasn't quite tall enough to reach. Just another few centimetres would do it.

Bracing one foot against a shelf, Sarah pushed herself up and grabbed for one of the overhead pipes. The spiders covering it dashed for safety and she was able to catch hold. With one foot on the shelf and one hand supporting her weight on the pipe, Sarah was easily able to reach the window. The rotten wood *squealed* as she heaved it all the way open, letting more light into the room.

She had just spotted the spray can when disaster struck. The pipe she was holding groaned, screeched, then broke with a *bang*. A jet of icy cold water shot from the end of it, blasting Sarah in the face. She fell backwards and hit the floor hard as the pipe continued to douse her like a fireman's hose.

At first, it was just the shock of the fall and the freezing cold water that bothered her, but then the enormity of what was happening hit her. The icy torrent was washing off the lavender. Her only protection from the spiders was being blasted away!

With a cough and a splutter, the water died away, but the damage was already done. As Sarah scrambled to her feet, a thousand fleeing spiders turned and swarmed straight for her.

Jake had silently debated the idea of fighting the Creeper and his giant spider. He didn't debate it for long though before coming to a very definite decision.

'Run for it!' he yelped, hurrying down the hillside with Liam bounding along beside him.

'Yes, flee!' the Creeper called after them, his laughter echoing through the night air. 'It makes it *so* much more fun when you try to escape.'

'Oh no,' Jake muttered, as he ran. 'We couldn't have just gone to Disneyland. You don't get giant spiders at Disneyland.'

'No,' Liam agreed. 'Although, I hear the mice there can get pretty big.'

From somewhere behind them, they heard the fast-paced thunder of lots of large legs on the grass. They dived apart just as the King of All Spiders launched itself through the air. It landed expertly and turned quickly, but Jake and Liam were already zigzagging away from it, arms and legs pumping as they hurtled down the hill.

Quite where they were going, neither of them knew. The exit would still be blocked, they knew, and they couldn't run forever.

'Look out,' Jake warned, pulling Liam aside just as the spider came flying through the air again. It slammed into a crumbling old gravestone, turning it to rubble, and then the chase was on again.

'Head for the house,' Jake suggested. It was the only thing he could think to do. Besides, he wanted to find Sarah. If they were all going to die, then it would be better for them all to die together.

Not *much* better, admittedly, but a little bit.

'You've got some sort of really clever, super cunning plan, right?' Liam asked.

'Yes,' said Jake. 'It's *don't get killed by a giant spider*. I'm still working on the details.'

Sarah knew there was no way she could get up the stairs, through the kitchen and out of the house without being buried alive by spiders. The lavender was completely washed off her now, and the spiders were closing fast. She was almost certainly done for, but she wasn't going to go down without a fight.

Scrambling to her feet, she snatched up the bug spray and gave the can a shake. No! It was barely half full. If she was going to use it to destroy the bush, she couldn't afford to waste much. But then, if she was going to use it on the bush, first she had to get out of here without being buried alive by squirming legs.

She spun on the spot, blasting a circle of spiders with the stuff. They immediately stopped running and began waving their legs in the air as the chemicals in the spray took effect.

'And let that be a lesson to the rest of you!' Sarah spat, then she raced towards her only chance of escape—the window. The shelf unit beside it wobbled unsteadily as she climbed up. Spiders scuttled and scurried over her hands and up her arms, but she gritted her teeth, ignored them, and tried not to freak out.

One of the bugs dropped from the ceiling and landed in her hair. Then another. And another. Sarah felt panic rising like a bubble inside her, but she forced it down. The boys needed her. Lower Larkspur-on-Sea needed her. Heck, maybe the whole *world* needed her.

Even if just for Jake and Liam's sake, she wasn't going to let a few creepy-crawlies stop her.

With a grunt of effort, she hoisted herself across from the shelves and caught hold of the window ledge. Then, with dozens of arachnids swarming over her, Sarah began to climb.

Jake and Liam were almost at the foot of the hill, charging across the grass, when they saw the figure come running towards them. They recognized Sarah at once, and Jake felt a wave of relief wash over him when he saw the spray can in her hand.

And then the relief was replaced by terror as Sarah suddenly fell forwards onto the grass, as if something had pushed her over.

'Sarah!' Liam yelped, finding an extra burst of speed tucked away somewhere inside his legs. He reached her just ahead of Jake, and began helping her to her feet. 'It's OK, sis, I've got you,' he said, then he spotted all the spiders crawling on her, and immediately dropped her again.

'Ow!' Sarah protested, as she thumped face-first onto the grass. 'What did you do that for?'

Liam stared at the bugs clambering all over Sarah's head and body. One of them was even creeping across her cheek. 'Um, you've got some spiders on you.'

'I know,' Sarah said, getting up and beginning to brush at her clothes.

'What happened?' asked Jake. 'I thought something had knocked you over.'

'I tripped on something in the grass,' Sarah said, but before they could investigate, a hiss rang out from somewhere over Jake's shoulder. The giant spider had caught up, and was lurking behind them, its long legs slowly picking their way through the overgrown grass.

'Quick, spray it with the bug stuff!' said Jake.

Sarah looked down at her hands. Empty. 'Oh no,' she gasped, her eyes darting over the dark, shadowy ground. 'I must have dropped the can when I fell.'

'Oh, now that *is* a shame,' sniggered a voice from the darkness. The Creeper emerged from the gloom, a wicked grin twisting his deformed, bark-like face. 'And just when it looked like you might actually stand a chance of messing up my plans. How very disappointing.' His grin widened. 'For you, I mean.'

Sarah's eyes widened and her mouth flopped open, then she remembered there were spiders on her face and closed it again. 'The Creeper,' she whispered.

'Oh, yeah,' said Liam. 'Jake was right. It's the

Creeper. Or maybe just someone who looks very like the Creeper?'

Jake shook his head. 'No. It's the Creeper.'

Liam shrugged. 'Ah well. Worth a try.'

'The genuine, bona fide, never to be repeated, one and only Master of Nature!' the Creeper announced, sweeping his long arms around in a dramatic gesture. 'It will be an honour for you to die at my command.'

The monster raised a hand and gestured towards the children. 'Kill them. Kill them all!'

The spider lurched towards them, its mandibles opening to reveal a mouth filled with terrifyingly sharp fangs.

'Liam, hit it!' Jake yelped.

'With what?'

Jake pointed to the branch, which was still clutched

in Liam's hand. 'Oh, yeah,' said Liam. 'Forgot about that.'

He swung at the bug, but a leg whipped up and knocked the stick away. Liam quickly jumped back.

'OK, that didn't work. Any other ideas?'

Running was the only other option, but when Jake glanced over his shoulder he saw the whole graveyard behind him glistening with the shiny black bodies of tens of thousands of spiders. Sarah was coping well with a couple of dozen on her, but a few thousand would be enough to take all three of the children down as they climbed into their airways and choked them with their tiny hairy bodies.

The reality of the situation hit Jake like a sledgehammer blow, knocking the wind from him. There was nowhere to run. No way to fight. This was it. This was the end.

Or was it? A black shape sailed through the night towards the spider. In the moonlight, Jake caught a glimpse of sharp teeth and sharper claws, and then the spider wrenched around, hissing in pain as the thing landed on its back and said, 'Miaow.'

The cat's claws tore at the join where the spider's head met its body. Teeth sank into the exposed muscle at one of the monster's many shoulders, and the spider squealed in pain.

'No!' roared the Creeper, making a dive for the cat. 'Get off it, you filthy little beast!'

As the Creeper tried to pull the cat away, it raked its claws across his bark-like face, scratching him across one of his glowing green eyes. He stumbled back, blinded, and the cat turned its attention back to the spider once more.

'It's protecting us!' said Liam. 'It's, like, Supercat, the fearless feline hero who—'

'I think it's trying to eat it,' Sarah said.

Liam pulled a face. 'Ew. That's disgusting.' He shrugged. 'Still, works for me.'

'Quick, help me find the spray,' Sarah said, turning and searching the grass.

'Found it!' said Liam, almost instantly. Jake and Sarah both cheered. 'Oh no, wait. I tell a lie. It's just a manhole cover.'

Sarah tutted. 'That must've been what I tripped over,' she said, then she and Jake both spotted the bug spray at the same time, and knocked heads as they dived to grab it.

One of the spiders on Sarah's head made a dash onto Jake's, and he frantically slapped himself as he tried to knock it away. 'Ugh, get off!'

'Calm down,' Sarah told him, plucking the arachnid from his hair. 'Don't be such a baby.'

'Thanks,' breathed Jake. It was great that Sarah was no longer scared of spiders, but at the same time he couldn't help but be a tiny bit disappointed. It had been nice to know she had some sort of weakness, but now she was back to being fantastic at everything again!

The spider and the cat were locked in battle now. The giant bug kicked and thrashed like a bucking bronco, trying desperately to throw the kitty off. The cat was managing to hold on with its claws for now, but as the spider's movements became more violent, it was only a matter of time before it lost its grip.

Jake looked down at the manhole cover. A plan was forming.

'Here, give me a hand with this,' he said, scrabbling at the edges of the circle of metal. Liam and Sarah both rushed to his side, and together they managed to raise the manhole lid, revealing a long drop into a deep, dark tunnel below.

Holding the manhole lid upright, they took cover behind it. Peeking out, they watched in growing horror as the Creeper caught the cat and managed to wrench it free. With a roar of rage, the monster tossed the flailing kitty far across the graveyard. It would land on its feet, Jake knew, but it'd probably think twice about taking on the spider again.

'Bang on the cover,' Jake said to Sarah. She frowned,

confused, but did it anyway. The metal spray can *clanged* against the lid like a gong.

'Come on, then!' Jake urged, beckoning to the bug. 'Come and get us.'

Sarah worked out the plan right away. She banged harder on the manhole cover, trying to get the spider's attention. 'Yeah, come and get us, you eight-legged weirdo.'

'Guys?! What are you doing?' Liam whimpered. 'Stop winding it up, it's angry enough as it is. You're only going to make it worse.'

Jake and Sarah ignored him. 'That's right!' Jake shouted. 'We're right here. What's the matter? You scared?'

The spider raced towards them, its legs thundering across the grass as it headed straight for the open manhole hidden in the grass. It was working. The plan was working!

'Wait!' said the Creeper, and the spider skidded to a stop just centimetres from the hole's edge. Jake's heart leaped into his throat. No! So close. They'd been so close.

The Creeper nodded approvingly. 'Nice try,' he said. 'You almost did it. You almost managed to trick my prize specimen into falling for your trap. But there's one thing you didn't count on. Me!'

Jake saw a movement on the hillside behind the Creeper. A fast-moving blur was streaking across the grass. He smiled. He couldn't help it.

'Oh yeah, well there's something you didn't count on, either,' Jake said. 'Him!'

Max raced between the Creeper's legs, barking and snarling at the spider with such ferocity it stumbled just a single step in surprise. That one step was enough, though. As it failed to notice the hole, the giant arachnid lost its balance. Its legs flailed and panic flashed across its glassy black eyes, and then it was falling, tumbling, plummeting down into the darkness of the sewer below.

CHAPTER THIRTEEN

FACE OFF

Even before the big spider had *splashed* into the murky water below, the smaller versions crawling all over Sarah all dropped onto the grass. She and the boys watched as the bugs raced towards the manhole and threw themselves in after their larger cousin.

The grass around them was suddenly heaving with a living carpet of the eight-legged critters. They flowed like a river, then became a waterfall as they all began plunging over the edge of the manhole.

'They're following the king. Or queen. Or whatever,' Sarah gasped.

Miaow!

The cat leaped into the mass of spiders, its teeth snapping as it tucked into the most disgusting all-you-can-eat buffet that Jake had ever seen. As the spiders poured down into the sewer, the cat leapt in after them, *miaowing* angrily as it plunged down into the dark.

'No! Stop!' the Creeper howled at his spider army. 'Get back here. Where are you going?!'

With the monster distracted, Jake, Sarah, and Liam let the manhole cover fall backwards, then raced up the hill towards the bush. The egg sacs were bulging and squirming furiously. The children may have got rid of one giant spider, but a whole platoon of them was about to be born.

'Go, go, go!' Jake cried, as Sarah ran for the bush, bug spray in hand. She blasted the first egg sac, coating it in a cloud of toxic chemicals. Almost at once, the squirming inside stopped, as the sac began to shrivel and dissolve.

One of the forest's trees turned suddenly. A branch whipped out, slamming into Sarah's side and sending her stumbling across the grass. The bug spray flew from her hand, but Liam snatched it from the air and blasted the next egg sac, destroying it just as Sarah had with the first one.

Before he could spray the third sac, though, a vine erupted through the grass, tangling around him and pinning his arms to his sides. He managed to toss the can to Jake just before he was trapped, and Jake made a desperate dash for the final sac.

The grass tugged at his feet. The bush itself stabbed at him with thin, sharp branches. But there was no way he was letting the Creeper stop him. He pushed on, ripping the grass from the ground until he reached the final spider sac.

This one was larger than the others. It had already begun to split open, and Jake caught a glimpse of hundreds of legs wriggling around in there before he pressed down on the top of the can and unleashed a concentrated blast of chemical death inside.

The monsters-to-be thrashed and squirmed and then, finally, their legs curled up beneath them as the egg sac shrivelled like an old prune.

From further down the hill there came a screech of pain and panic and despair. At first, Jake thought the spiders must have overpowered the poor cat, but then he spotted the source of the sound. The Creeper was rushing up the hillside towards them, screaming at the top of his voice.

'No! What have you done? What have you done?!' he roared. 'Why do you always have to interfere?'

147

'To be fair, you *were* trying to kill us,' Sarah pointed out.

'We've stopped you again, Creeper,' said Jake. Sarah limped over to stand by his side. Liam half-shuffled, half-hopped, most of him still wrapped in the vine.

'Ymf! Eev omped oo, eefar,' Liam added, although with his face partially covered in vines, no one understood a word of what he said.

The Creeper's face was a mask of absolute fury. He flicked his hands, extending ten long, twig-like claws from his fingertips. 'No, you stopped my spiders!' the monster snarled. 'You haven't stopped me, though. You'll *never* stop—'

Jake emptied the last of the bug spray into the Creeper's face in one big squirt. Instantly, the villain leaped back, shrieking and sobbing and desperately trying to wipe the stuff away. 'My eyes!' he howled. 'My face! My beautiful face!'

The children had no idea what sort of chemicals were in the spray, but they clearly weren't very good for plants. As the Creeper stumbled backwards, his bark-like skin began to sizzle and melt. He lashed out wildly, but was several metres away from Jake and the others, and heading in the wrong direction.

'W-water!' he sobbed. 'I need water.'

The grass beneath his feet rose up like a platform

and carried him swiftly towards the open sewer. Even from this distance, Jake could see that spiders were still tumbling into the hole in their thousands. Just how many of the things had been lurking around here?!

'I'll get you for this!' the Creeper hissed. 'You haven't heard the last of meeeeeeeeee!'

The last word came out as a long, drawn-out scream as the genuine, bona fide, never to be repeated, one and only Master of Nature tumbled down the manhole and landed in the murky brown water with a *splash*.

The vines that had wrapped around Liam fell away. 'Looks like that's the Creeper's evil plan down the drain,' Liam said.

Sarah groaned. 'You've been waiting ages to say that, haven't you?'

Liam nodded. 'Since the spider fell in, yeah. Good one, wasn't it?'

Jake put his arm around his friend's shoulder and grinned. 'For you, Liam, it wasn't actually half bad.'

Woof!

The three friends looked down to see Max sitting on the ground in front of them, his tongue hanging out, his tail thumping excitedly against the grass. Jake scooped him up and patted him. 'Good boy, Max. We couldn't have done it without you.'

'Looks like the path's clear,' said Sarah, peering into

149

the gloom. 'We can get out of here. We should go and get your mum and dad.'

Jake nodded. The path was clear, but the cottage would still be full of spiders. He wasn't quite sure how he'd explain it to his parents, but it'd have to be done sooner or later.

'Come on, then,' he said. 'Let's go and fill them in.'

Jake stood outside the front door with his hand on the handle. Liam and Sarah stood either side of him, with Mum and Dad standing on the path. It was completely clear of creepy-crawlies, which was a bonus, but the house would be a different story.

'OK, so brace yourselves,' he warned. 'This will come as a bit of a shock.'

'Just hurry up,' said Dad, shivering. 'It's freezing out here.'

Jake glanced at his friends, who both nodded, then pushed the door open. Dad and Mum both gasped in disbelief.

'*Good grief!*' said Jake's dad. 'It's still in one piece.'

'And tidy, too,' said Mum, stepping past Jake into the hallway. The completely spider-free hallway. She

150

looked around. 'I was sure you'd have made a mess of the place.'

Jake and the others peered into the hall, searching for bugs, but finding none.

'Don't speak too soon,' said Dad, striding past them. 'We haven't seen the rest of the house yet.'

He pushed open the kitchen door, then let out a high-pitched squeal and jumped back in fright. 'Argh! What is *that*?'

Jake, Liam, and Sarah dashed down the hall and skidded to a stop at the kitchen. The back door stood open, and a familiar mangy-looking black cat sat in the middle of the kitchen floor. Dangling from its mouth was a long, slender spider-leg, easily half a metre from top to bottom. It looked like the King of All Spiders hadn't made a clean getaway through the sewers, after all.

The cat purred happily, then about-turned and trotted back out into the garden, dragging its prize with it.

Jake grinned. 'Oh, it's nothing. Just a local cat,' he said.

'No, not the cat, I know what a cat is!' said Dad. 'But what was that in its mouth?'

Jake walked into the kitchen, closed the door, then turned to his dad and shrugged. 'No idea,' he said, smiling. 'But something tells me it's not something we have to worry about.'

CHAPTER FOURTEEN

HACKER'S FAREWELL

So, there you have it. Now you know the real story of that spider found in the supermarket.

Oh, wait, no, you don't. After I interviewed the children, I think I've been able to piece it together.

Although first appearances suggested all the spiders had left the house, that wasn't quite true. That night, as Liam was about to get into bed, he found one of the creepy-crawlies perching on the ladder of the bunk beds. It was a pretty big one—not enormous, like the monster-spider, of course, but big enough—and it refused to budge. After the day they'd had, both Liam and Jake

153

were—understandably, I think—reluctant to touch it.

Luckily for them, Sarah heard Liam's screams. She swooped in, carefully picked the spider up, then calmly released it into the garden.

Based on the direction it headed, the time of night it happened, and the time the supermarket spider was discovered, I'd guess both spiders were one and the same, although it's impossible for me to be sure. A few more spiders were discovered dotted around the town over the following few days, so it's safe to say that although most of its little minions followed the big one down into the sewer, a few of them stayed behind.

Thankfully, though, the real danger was over. Lower Larkspur-on-Sea—and very possibly the whole world—had been saved, and it was all thanks to the bravery of Jake, Sarah, and Liam.

I went back to Lower Larkspur-on-Sea a few weeks later. The holiday house—the childhood home of the Creeper himself—was empty, and there were no spiders to be seen anywhere. The church cat was looking particularly well-fed, though, and had put on quite a lot of weight between then and when I first covered the story.

Well-fed or not, there was no way one cat could have eaten all those arachnids, which means—just like the Creeper—they're all still out there, somewhere.

So, next time you spy a spider crawling across your ceiling, or scurrying across the kitchen floor, be careful. It might just be one of the Creeper's eight-legged pets. And this time, it might be coming for you.

Your friend,
Hacker Murphy

ARE YOU BRAVE ENOUGH
TO FIND OUT HOW THE

CREEPER FILES

BEGAN?

READ ON FOR A TASTE OF

THE ROOT OF ALL EVIL.

AVAILABLE NOW.

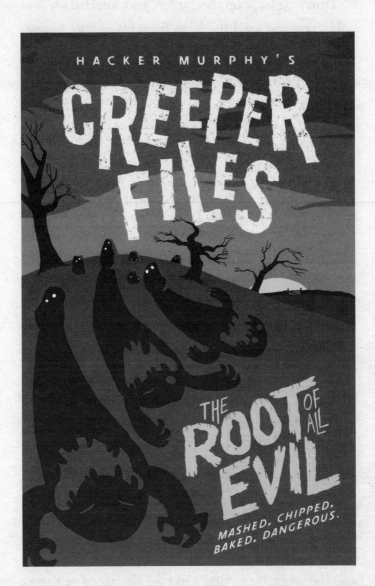

HACKER MURPHY'S

CREEPER FILES

THE ROOT OF ALL EVIL

MASHED. CHIPPED.
BAKED. DANGEROUS.

Hurrying back up the garden, Jake kneeled on the cold grass and used the light from his mobile phone to check on his mum's budding flowers—but they weren't there. Instead, he found a handful of torn green leaves and the occasional pink or purple petal.

'Oh no,' said Jake to himself. 'Not again!'

Three times now in the past six weeks, someone had attacked gardens in this neighbourhood at night, tearing up flower beds, and generally ruining all the hard work put into their greenery by his mum and all their neighbours.

At first, blame was laid directly at the feet of young ruffians. The young ruffians quickly got together to issue a statement in which they denied any involvement in the garden-wrecking, and threatened to kick the heads in of anyone who said different. After that, everyone stopped pointing the finger their way.

Jake stood up and peered out into the darkness of the street, searching for—well, something that looked suspicious. The trouble was that everything looked suspicious in the fizzing yellow glow of the ancient street lamps. Even Dad's tool shed on the far side of the lawn had a distinct air of malice about it at night, and the worst thing that had ever happened in there was the time Dad's barrel of home brew ginger beer had exploded while he was testing the mixture. It took over a week of showers before the local cats would stop following him everywhere he went.

Glancing back at the house, Jake briefly considered heading back inside to tell his mum what had happened, but knew she wouldn't be happy if he didn't take Max out on his walk first. He fished a slightly crushed bag of salt and vinegar crisps out of his pocket and tore it open, eager to rid his taste buds of the lingering aftermath of broccoli. He tipped the bag up to his mouth, when—

CRASH!

The sound had come from further down the street. Could the flower-flattening fiend still be here? Still up to his wicked work? There was only one way to find out ...

Easing the gate open, Jake slipped the crisp packet back into his pocket and allowed Max to lead him out into the street. The dog pulled and pulled, something he would normally be told off for, but on this occasion Jake welcomed both Max's keen nose, and the fact that he could look quite big and scary under the right lights—and these were indeed the right lights.

So he let Max tug him along the road in the direction of the sound. Jake peered over walls and fences as they hurried along. Each one had been attacked by whoever—or whatever—was doing this. Plants had been torn up at the roots and scattered over lawns. Snapped stems and pulverized petals were all that remained of carefully tended flower beds. And, in one garden, the little gnome sitting at the edge of the pond had had his fishing rod snapped in half.

Was there no end to the evil currently stalking Larkspur?

Max picked up the pace. Jake could feel his heart pumping in his chest, and his palms were growing sweaty. Quite what he would do if he did stumble across a gang of motorbike-owning, tulip-despising ne'er-do-wells he didn't rightly know. Maybe it was time to arrange some backup.

Grabbing his mobile phone from his pocket, he hit speed-dial 2, clamped the phone to his ear, and tried to hear the ringing sound over the noise of Max's excited panting.

Eventually, the line connected with a CLICK!

'Liam,' Jake hissed. 'It's me.'

'Jake-a-roo!' cried Liam's tinny voice through the phone's speaker. 'I was expecting you to call . . .'

'You were?'

'Obviously! I mean—come on . . . You must have installed the new power pack for *Brick-Quest* by now! What do you think of it?'

Jake sighed. Of course. This evening was when the latest upgrade to their favourite computer game was due to be released. With the battle of the broccoli—and now a potential monster on the loose—he'd forgotten all about it.

'Well . . .'

'Tell me you've at least downloaded it!'

'Sorry, no . . .' said Jake. 'I'm out at the moment, walking Max.'

'Running Max by the sounds of it mate, you're out of breath.'

'Yeah,' gasped Jake. 'He's really going for it tonight.'

'So, if it's not to tell me that *Brick-Quest 2.8* is the best version of the game ever, why did you ring me?'

'It's the gardens again,' said Jake, 'they're—'

He stopped as Max's ears flattened back and he began to growl softly.

'What is it, boy?' hissed Jake, peering into the darkness.

And then he saw it. Standing in the next-to-last garden of the street was a tall, extremely thin figure, silhouetted in the harsh yellow streetlight on the corner. The man—and it had to be a man—bent over and Jake could hear the unmistakable sound of flower stems breaking as the figure tore them from the ground.

Then slowly, deliberately, the man raised the handful of tattered blooms to his mouth—and he began to eat them. The figure chewed carefully as though he was savouring the flavours of a gourmet meal.

Then, Max barked. The man's head jerked in their direction, tendrils of half-eaten greenery dangling from between his teeth. Then he turned and started to walk towards them.

Pulling hard on Max's lead, Jake swung open the nearest garden gate and led his pet down onto a well-maintained lawn beyond. Like the other gardens, ruined flower beds said the thin man had been here as well, presumably making a meal of the owner's hard work. But he hadn't touched a thick hedge standing sentry near the front door of the house. Warning Max to stay silent, Jake pulled him behind the hedge.

The tall, thin man came closer—easing his way along the street while finishing off his fistful of flowers. Jake still couldn't make them out, but he could tell that the man's eyes were sweeping the shadows, searching for him. The creature was sniffing at the air too, as though he could discern the scent of living flesh from partially-devoured foliage.

All Jake had to do was stay absolutely silent, and he would be—

BEEP BEEP! BEEP BEEP!

Jake stared in horror as a text message lit up the screen of his phone. It was from Liam . . .

'You can design your own bricks!'

The figure spun to look straight at Jake. And this time he could see the figure's eyes.

They were glowing bright green.

Max began to bark furiously, pulling at his lead, desperate to be free.

The figure glared down at the angry dog, seemingly unconcerned.

'Don't come any closer!' Jake warned. 'Max can be very . . . bitey when he feels threatened.'

Bitey?! Jake thought to himself. *You're not exactly talking tough here. You might as well say he does big woof-woofs!*

Then the figure lifted a long leg, and started to climb over the garden wall.

Jake backed away even further. 'I mean it!' he said, trying to stop his voice from trembling. 'Stay back, or I'll let him off the lead!'

But the shadowy figure didn't stay back. With its piercing eyes still fixed on Jake, it stepped completely over the wall and started to cross the lawn.

Then it reached out towards him with one of its arms, long twig-like fingers twisting and turning. The monster gurgled, almost as though it were laughing.

'OK!' cried Jake, swallowing his fear. 'You asked for it!'

His own fingers trembling, Jake unclipped the lead from Max's collar. 'Go on boy!' he hissed into his pet's ear. 'Do your worst!'

Both Jake and the dark figure watched as Max sped across the lawn, leapt over the wall, and then raced down the street in the direction of home.

There was a brief silence while both parties processed what had happened.

'Thanks a lot, pal!' Jake shouted after his rapidly-disappearing dog.

Then the tall, thin figure continued its journey across the lawn towards him.

'Right!' Jake said, his voice cracking. 'Slight change of plan. Come one step closer, and I'm calling the police!'

The figure came one step closer.

'Two steps closer, then!' cried Jake. 'Two steps, and I'll dial 999!'

The figure took another step towards the terrified boy.

'Three steps!' shouted Jake. 'That's my absolute final offer! I'm really good at playing *Brick-Quest Lite* on here, so you won't believe how fast I can dial the number for the emergency services!'

One more step.

'Why won't you listen?' yelled Jake, his back pressed

against the front door of the house behind him.

Suddenly, the security light above the door lit up, flooding the garden with the glare of a hundred white LED bulbs. *I must have triggered the sensor*, Jake thought to himself. He looked back at the creature who was still advancing.

Jake's thumb hammered down on the first 9 of the emergency number, but his hand was trembling so hard that he somehow dropped his phone.

'No!' he cried, eyes searching the grass at his feet. But he was still seeing swirls of colours from looking directly into the security light, and he couldn't find his mobile anywhere.

He rifled through his pockets, desperate to find another weapon with which to ward off this horrifying half-man.

All he had was a packet of salt and vinegar crisps.

It would have to do.

Plunging his hand down into the pack, he grasped a few fingerfuls of the salty snacks and hurled them directly at his advancing attacker's face.

To his amazement, the monster lurched back as they landed. Long, spindly fingers shot up to rub the crispy crumbs off whatever this thing had for skin, and the creature wailed in agony.

'Ha!' cried Jake, tossing more crisps at the bellowing beast. 'Thought you could attack me and get away with it, did you?'

The thing staggered back even further, hands raised to save itself from the onslaught of the deep-fried potato product.

Jake waited until he was sure the figure was too far away to suddenly reach out and grab him, then he, like Max before him, leapt over the garden wall and raced along the street for home.

'Glowing green eyes?' said Liam.

Jake nodded. 'They practically lit up the entire garden. Well, that and the security light. It's where I dropped my phone.'

Liam's sister, Sarah, paused to look over a wall at yet another scene of devastation. 'Which garden was it?'

'No idea,' said Jake with a shrug. 'Bit of a lawn, lots of torn up flowers . . .'

'That describes just about all of them.'

'There was quite a big hedge,' said Jake, recalling his hiding place. 'That should narrow it down a bit.'

'Why do we want to know which garden Jake was

in?' asked Liam.

'I'd quite like my phone back,' Jake said.

'Oh,' said Liam. 'Yeah, fair point, well made.'

Sarah pulled a small plastic tub from her lunch bag and tore off the lid. 'Here,' she said to her brother. 'Want this?'

Liam gaped at a big wedge of chocolate and icing. 'Isn't that the cake you got at Eliza's birthday yesterday?'

'Yes,' said Sarah. 'But I need the tub.'

'Ace!' Liam beamed, grabbing the gateau and stuffing it into his mouth. 'Breakfast cake!'

Sarah tapped the empty container on a garden wall to get rid of the crumbs. 'I thought we could get a sample from the flowers this creature was eating,' she said. 'Then we could take it into the science lab and ask Professor Bloom to test it under a microscope.'

'Why would we ask Professor Bloom?' Liam wondered.

Sarah rolled her eyes. 'Because she's a botanist. She knows about plants.'

'Oh yeah,' said Liam, spraying cake crumbs everywhere. 'Another good point, well made.'

'Whoa, whoa . . .' said Jake, holding up a hand. 'We're not telling teachers or anyone else about what I saw! Especially not the deputy head!'

'Why not?' asked Sarah.

'Well, one—it makes me sound like a right head-case and, two—I ran away from the thing. In terror.'

'He's right,' said Liam, spraying yet more crumbs down his jumper. 'You don't go around school saying that you met a real life monster and then you ran away.'

'Well, I did,' Jake admitted. 'And you would have done, too.'

Liam shook his head. 'Not me. Anyway, I was right where I should have been, at home playing the new *Brick-Quest* upgrade. Isn't it brilliant?'

Jake shrugged. 'I've no idea!'

'What? You still haven't downloaded it?'

'I haven't had a chance!' cried Jake. 'Once I'd told my mum what had happened, she got me in the car and dragged me down to the police station to make a report.'

'What kind of report?'

'She reckoned I was just seconds away from being mugged.'

'By a tree?'

Jake stared back at his friend. 'You're not helping.'

'Sorry!' said Liam. 'But, you did tell her the twigs-for-fingers part, and the trailing roots, and the glowing green eyes, didn't you?'

'Of course!' said Jake. 'Well, a bit. By the time I got

home I was starting to wonder whether I'd actually seen all that stuff, or if I was just suffering the side effects of a broccoli overdose.'

'You didn't describe this creature to the police at all?' asked Sarah.

'I tried,' said Jake. 'Well, my mum made me try. I got to the bit where I told them I'd managed to fight it off by throwing salt and vinegar crisps in its face and they stopped writing things down.'

'What?' said Liam. 'They didn't believe you?'

Jake shook his head. 'Mum took me back home and made me a cup of beetroot and chive tea. She said it was the best thing for someone in shock.'

'Ooh,' said Liam, wincing. 'More vegetables. Not a good result.'

'Tell me about it,' said Jake. 'So, no . . . we're not going to tell Professor Bloom what I saw last night.'

'OK,' said Sarah. 'We won't tell Professor Bloom . . .'

'Or anyone else . . .' Jake added.

Sarah nodded. 'Or anyone else. We'll go to the lab at break time and use one of the microscopes ourselves.'

'I can't do break time,' said Liam. 'Got a game of football against the year nines. Gonna be a belter, too.'

'Right, then,' said Sarah with a sigh. 'Jake and I will use one of the microscopes. If we can find any samples of the flowers the thing was eating.'

'Wait,' said Jake, stopping at a garden and peering over the wall. Like all the others in the street, its flower beds had been destroyed. 'This could be it. The house has got a security light, and there's a big hedge to hide behind.'

'And this is where you dropped your phone and shared your crisps with a monster?'

'No,' said Jake, 'this is where I hurled my crisps at an advancing nightmare that looked as though it wanted to suck my brain out through my ears! But yes, I dropped my phone.'

'Hang on,' said Liam, pulling out his own phone. 'We'll soon find it . . .' He quickly dialled a number, and then all three of them leaned in towards the garden and listened.

The theme tune from *Brick-Quest* began to play. It sounded muted and distant, as if it was far away.

'That's it!' cried Jake, straining his ears. 'My phone!' He swung open the gate and darted across the lawn towards the thick hedge where he had been hiding the night before . . .

. . . when the front door to the house swung open and an angry-looking man emerged. He had a bald head, and was wearing a baggy, off-white vest.

'This your phone?' he demanded.

Jake looked up from the ground to see what the

man was holding.

'Yes,' he said with a grin. 'Did you find it out here this morning?'

'That's exactly what I did,' said the man. 'Along with what's left of my flower beds.'

'I know,' said Jake, surveying the damage. 'Terrible stuff.'

Suddenly, a horrible thought washed over him.

'Wait, you don't think it was *me* that did all this, do you?'

The man held up Jake's phone, which was still playing its jaunty ringtone. 'Well, this is evidence that you were here, isn't it?'

'Maybe not,' said Liam, wandering over to join Jake.

The man looked up at him. 'Eh?'

'You've got no proof that's Jake's phone at all!'

'Yes I have,' snarled the man. 'I was watching you through the window. You dialled a number on your phone, and his phone started to ring. That's how it works.'

'Fair enough,' said Liam with a sigh. 'You've got us.'

'No, he hasn't!' spat Jake. 'OK, yes—that's my phone, but it doesn't mean I was the one who ripped up all your plants and flowers.'

'So, what *were* you doing in my garden last night?'

'He was throwing crisps at some kind of—' said

Liam, quickly followed by 'OW!' as Jake kicked him in the shin. 'What did you do that for?'

'Sorry,' said Jake. 'I think I must have slept funny. Got a bit of a twitch in my leg today.'

He smiled pleasantly at the man in the vest. 'Yeah, I was here last night, walking my dog.'

Liam frowned. 'I thought Max came home by hims—OUCH!'

The man frowned. 'Do you normally walk your dog in other people's gardens?'

'Don't be daft!' chuckled Liam. 'He was in there hiding from—YEOW! Is there any chance you can make your leg twitch in a different direction, mate? I'm going to have a bruise there!'

The man fixed Jake with a stare. 'Go on. You were in my garden, hiding from . . .'

' . . . my dog,' said Jake, as matter-of-factly as he could. 'We were playing hide-and-seek.'

The man blinked. 'I'm sorry, did you just say you were in here playing hide-and-seek with your dog?'

'Yep!' said Jake.

'And, is your dog any good at playing hide-and-seek?' he asked.

'Nope!' said Jake. 'I found him almost straight away.'

'Does he play any other games, your dog?'

'Not really,' said Jake, shaking his head.

'No, just that,' said Sarah at the same time.

'Monopoly!' exclaimed Liam with a grin, which quickly faded when he caught his sister and best friend staring at him. 'Although he gets upset if you don't award him £10 for coming second in the beauty contest.'

'So, can I have my phone back, please?'

'Yeah, but I don't want to see any of you in my garden again!' The man handed the mobile back to its owner and disappeared back indoors.

Jake hit a key to silence the ringtone. 'Come on,' he said, walking away. 'We don't want to be late for school. We've got that new head teacher starting today.'

Liam followed, licking cake crumbs from his fingertips.

'Oh yeah,' said Sarah, 'I'd forgotten about him'. She stooped to grab her school bag and, when she was certain no one was watching through the window, she scooped some of the partially chewed vegetation into her plastic tub.

Then she hurried after the boys.

'I wonder what he'll be like?'

LARKSPUR
POLICE

REPORT COMPILED BY: *Sgt Pamela Holgate*

DATE: *25th March*

TIME: *9.40p.m.*

Mrs Anna Latchford of 10 Duncan Street, Larkspur attended the station with her son Jake (13), claiming that he had been the victim of a personal attack while out walking the family dog, Max (age unknown).

At first Jake was reluctant to describe his attacker, causing me to wonder if he feared reprisals should an arrest eventually be made.

However, it soon became clear that the boy was making it up as he went along, describing

a <u>seven-foot-tall plant</u> monster with green
eyes that he had managed to escape from by
<u>throwing crisps</u> (salt and vinegar).

REPORT COMPLETED: *10.02 P.M.*

Garden
destroyer
caught in the
act?

Seven feet
tall?

Fancy dress
costume?

Crisps as
Kryptonite!

Finally, after a session of double French that seemed to last an eternity, the bell rang for break time.

Liam leapt out of his chair, stuffing his exercise book into his bag as he sprinted for the door. He'd been looking forward to this match against the year nines all weekend. Lee 'Curly' Harper had been getting too big for his boots lately—football or otherwise—and scoring a few goals past him before it was time for geography would be very satisfying indeed. If he could get in the game.

At the start of the term they had tried letting everyone who showed up join in, but it turned out that thirty-seven players on each team didn't improve the game of football at all. In fact, if anything, it rather ruined things. Especially for Billy Salter, who was driven away in an ambulance with at least three different players' shoe prints coming up as bruises on his freshly broken leg.

It was back to eleven-a-side after that.

Liam crashed through the doorway to the stairs, taking them four at a time and yelling at a clutch of tiny year sevens to get out of his way.

He hit daylight, and his heart sank. There were

dozens of kids already lining up at the edge of the football pitch. There was no way he was going to get picked for the game now. It was bad enough that they only got fifteen minutes for break each morning—matches had to be seven minutes each way, with a minute spare to argue over whose turn it was to take the ball all the way back to the sports cupboard afterwards.

But, when he reached the edge of the playing field, Liam was amazed to see that no one was playing football at all. In fact, no one *could* play football. Because there was a huge red tractor busy ploughing the pitch up into long, even rows.

'What's going on?' he demanded.

'Dunno,' said Sickly Terry from year nine, spinning the ball in his hands. 'Looks like Woody's having some sort of breakdown.'

Liam peered closer at the tractor and saw that it was being driven by Professor Bloom's lab assistant, Woody Hemlock.

'I bet it all ends in a police chase,' said Sickly Terry.

'You what?'

'There's this programme I watch on telly,' Terry explained, '*Police, Camera, Edit That Bit Out* it's called. These things always end in a police chase down the motorway at 90 miles per hour.'

'But, Woody's driving a tractor . . .'

'Alright, 20 miles per hour.'

'This is ridiculous!' barked Liam. 'I'm going to find out what's going on!'

Stepping out onto what had once been a beautiful football pitch, Liam felt his shoes sink into the soil of the freshly-furrowed field as he marched towards the tractor.

'You, boy!' cried a voice.

Liam turned, squinting against the sunlight to make out a tall man with a bald head and large, bristly moustache on the touchline. He was wearing a bright tracksuit and white trainers that had been cleaned to within an inch of their lives.

And he was jogging on the spot.

Liam had no idea who it was and, judging by the looks of his fellow footballers, neither did they.

'Er . . . did you want something, mate?'

The man beamed. 'Yes!' he cried out. 'I'd like to give you the opportunity to run five laps around the school with me!'

Liam opened his mouth to reply, but the man was already sprinting away.

'Come on, laddie!' he shouted over his shoulder. 'The sooner you start, the sooner we're all fighting fit!'

As the rest of the gathered pupils began to giggle, Liam reluctantly gave chase.

Ready for more great stories?
Try one of these...

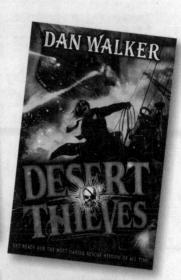